Triple

by

Stephanie Brother

**A REVERSE HAREM
STEPBROTHER ROMANCE**

Triplet Time © 2018 Stephanie Brother

All Rights Reserved. This book or any portion thereof may not be reproduced or used in any manner whatsoever without the express permission of the publisher except for the use of brief quotations in a book review.

This book is a work of fiction. Any resemblance to persons, living or dead, or places, events or locations is purely coincidental. The characters are all productions of the author's imagination.

Please note that this work is intended only for adults over the age of 18 and all characters represented as 18 or over.

Book cover designed by Silver Heart Publishing.

www.facebook.com/stephaniebrother

CHAPTER ONE
SOPHIE

I could barely take my eyes off his dick. It was rude to stare, but what else could I do?

I never expected to see my stepbrother naked like that. Not when I was in a room with twelve other people. Of course, I never expected to see it at all under any circumstances.

When asked to adopt a comfortable standing position for five minutes, Carl dropped the bathrobe without any sign of hesitation.

Not that he had anything to be shy about.

With the physique of a Greek god, he stood at over six feet tall with massive biceps and broad shoulders. He was ripped and well proportioned. Very well proportioned, as it turned out.

His thick cock hung halfway to his knees. Okay, that might be an exaggeration, but not by much. He stood still long enough for me to measure it, utilizing the usual method.

With one eye shut and my pencil held out in front of me, I assessed the length of his flaccid dick in relation to his torso and his legs. That was the usual technique for working out proportions in these art classes.

When I turned up to the life drawing class, I thought the model would probably be someone a lot older, not so attractive, and definitely not someone I knew.

Not my stepbrother.

But there he stood, just a few feet away, with his legs slightly apart and hands on hips. His big thick cock… thankfully, hanging down.

Like a relaxing pet python.

My eyes were drawn to it more than they should have been.

Imagine it standing up.

Oh. God. No. I did *not* need that mental image. I should *not* imagine it erect.

Too late. My brain had gone there.

I was sure my face flushed purple, and I felt as if I'd choke. I stooped down behind my easel for a moment of respite from the visual stimulation.

My nether regions were becoming hot and wet. How wrong was that? Very wrong, I figured. Wrong because this was a respectable life drawing class and wrong because that guy was my stepbrother, and I lived with him. I sat next to him for breakfast on weekends. The previous weekend we went to art exhibitions together. And now, he was exhibiting himself.

We'd been living in the same apartment for a few weeks, so I'd seen him topless before. Or had I? I couldn't be certain without giving it some thought.

I'd certainly seen one or two of the triplets without their tops. But they looked so alike that when I first moved in, I had difficulty telling them apart. And I tried hard not to pay too much attention when they exposed so much skin.

Well, once I'd clocked that all three were fine specimens of male beauty, I tried not to gaze at them at all if they had their tops off.

The artist in me wanted to look, of course. It was fascinating how much they were so alike as triplets, and it inspired many creative ideas.

The red-blooded woman in me wanted to look, too. To examine and touch and be touched.

Since moving into their apartment, I'd lost track of how many times I'd imagined one of them as my first. My first proper boyfriend. My first lover. I knew I shouldn't think like that about them. They were my stepbrothers. And there were three of them.

And as I'd gotten to know Carl better, I'd taken him from fantasy boyfriend land and put him into real-life best friend territory. That only left his enigmatic near-identical looking brothers for my dirty fantasies. A woman did not ogle their best friend's naked body. Just... no.

My thoughts were so wrong.

Even then, as I considered the best technique to reproduce the appearance and texture of his dark pubes, I began to crosshatch for three-dimensional depth. It was the shadow his dick cast against his thigh that held my fascination. I wanted to study it. Closely.

To understand my situation, you need to know that I'd only met my triplet stepbrothers on a few brief occasions before moving into their apartment. I lived with them because I moved to the city of Arlington to start art college.

It wasn't as if they were my actual brothers. We didn't grow up together.

I should explain the story from the beginning.

From the day I moved into their apartment, I just knew there'd be trouble.

CHAPTER TWO
CARL

"Where are Adam and Ben?" My father looked around the living room as if expecting them to jump out from behind the sofa. He knew well enough my brothers would do that sort of thing if they were here.

By mere minutes, Adam and Ben were my older brothers.

I was the last born of the Cooper triplets, but not the youngest child in the family. We have a much younger sister, Diana.

"They've stepped out for a while, and they'll be back soon. They thought Sophie might like to settle in without the place being too crowded with people." Dad and I had left Sophie in her new bedroom to unpack her stuff with her mother lending a hand. They didn't need our help.

Sophie's dad died when she was young, and so did our mom. That was one thing we had in common.

Barbara was Sophie's mom, and my dad's new wife. They'd known each other for years. They'd met through working together; well, my dad was her boss. She was an administrative assistant in his law practice, and they only recently married. It made Sophie our younger stepsister.

My father walked over to the window and gazed out at the magnificent view. "Then I have to ask, why are you still here?" He didn't look at me, but I was the only other person in the room.

Good question. As the official owner of the penthouse apartment, my dad had a key. He didn't need me here to let him in.

"I thought one of us should be here to greet her. She might have questions." I wandered over to the tiny kitchen area, which took up a corner of the living space.

He could have taken issue with my comment about the apartment feeling too crowded. It had five bedrooms and five bathrooms, and I'd only shared with my two brothers until now. It shouldn't feel crowded when six people were at home; however, there were limited places to hide. The bedrooms and bathrooms were the only private spaces, and everywhere else was open plan.

"Good. I'm pleased you're showing Sophie some consideration."

"I didn't want her to feel unwelcome. It would've seemed weird if none of us were here."

Dad hummed and sighed. "Barbara is worried about her oldest daughter leaving home, and we're trusting you boys to look after her."

"We'll look after her like as if she were our younger sister, you can be sure of that, Dad." I turned toward the fridge and opened the door to hide my reddening face.

My thoughts about her were not the thoughts any guy would have about a younger sister. At least we weren't related by blood, and we'd never lived together.

Until now.

I felt glad for the cooling air wafting over my flushed skin. "Can I get you a drink?" I asked, speaking into the cold space, and wanting to hide my flushed face behind it and have the cool air blowing on my heated skin.

Lying to my father didn't come easy, but I couldn't tell him what Adam, Ben, and I really said when we discussed Sophie.

Of course, as three guys in our early twenties, our *private* conversations went places that were best kept private. Let's say; we were frank with each other.

When it came to Sophie, we were all of the same mind; perhaps it was down to our shared genes. I wouldn't say our thoughts were lewd and disgusting, although there was an element of that.

Sophie was a babe to look at, a sweetie to talk to, and she was moving into our apartment.

Mostly, she was the sort of girl we each wanted to date and get to know better. Not just get her naked and fuck her every which way. But of course, we wanted to do that too.

We'd joked about competing for attention; winner takes all. We'd also discussed sharing her, and that was one hell of a hot fantasy. Three guys to satisfy our woman because she was too much for anyone on his own.

We didn't think of her in the same way as we should a sister.

Nevertheless, we brothers intended to behave like gentlemen and do all we could for her. One way or another.

Ultimately, it would be down to Sophie if she was interested in any of us. We weren't the sort of guys to become freaky scary roommates. We weren't going to stalk her or invade her privacy. We didn't want to make her feel uncomfortable and unsafe while she lived here with us. After all, we would be family for a long time into the future.

And even though we had dirty minds, we were basically decent guys.

"I don't want a drink. I'll wait until we go to the restaurant," Dad replied.

"Just orange juice for me then." Feeling a little more together, I picked up a carton and put it on the counter. I shut the fridge door and poured myself a glass of juice.

"I'd like to go to dinner early. We have a long drive ahead of us, and we want to get home at a reasonable time. Do you want to contact your brothers and tell them to get their asses back here?" He seemed a little pissed that they weren't here already.

My brothers should've stayed in because we knew the folks were coming.

"Shall I use my triplet telepathy, or shall I just use the phone?" I chuckled. Dad could contact them directly just as easily as me.

"Whichever works best." Dad simply shrugged; he didn't even chuckle at my joke. As far as he was concerned, all the triplet jokes had worn thin, many years ago.

"I'll make the call." I pulled the phone from the back pocket of my jeans and shot off a text to Ben.

: *You need to get home.*

A reply came back instantly: *Why?*

: *Dad wants to go to dinner soon. ETA? I replied.*

: *When are we going?*

As dad was the other side of the room and not looking over my shoulder, I replied.

: *The sooner we eat, the sooner we get back home. The sooner Dad is gone.*

He understood the implication. I didn't need to spell it out.

The sooner our dad and Sophie's mom left, the better. Sophie could start settling in properly, and we could get to know her better.

We weren't totally ungrateful. If it weren't for our dad, we wouldn't live in this luxurious penthouse apartment. We loved the old man, and any other time it would be great to have him visit and take us to dinner.

But it seemed weird having our parents hanging around after Sophie arrived because she was both one hot chick and also almost a stranger to us.

The three of us had lived together our entire lives and never lived with anyone else our age, so we were all eager to get to know her a little better and work out how she'd fit in with us in our house.

"There you are." Barbara's voice pulled me from my thoughts. "The woman's work is done. We've made Sophie's bed and unpacked her clothes. It's all looking far more feminine and homey in there already."

I looked up to see Sophie appearing a little sheepish as she followed her mom from her bedroom.

"Can I get you ladies a drink?" I was still standing at the kitchen island by the fridge.

"Yes, please, that would be lovely. Iced tea if you have it?" Barbara strode across the apartment toward me.

Sophie nodded. "The same for me, or something cold." She shut her bedroom door and leaned against it. I didn't know why.

She may have felt defensively protective of her new private domain and perhaps wanted to get back in there. Or she didn't want to join us by walking the length of the hall.

All five bedroom doors opened out on to a wide space that we called the hallway, but there were no doors separating it from the living area, and it was in clear view of the kitchen.

Discreetly sneaking guests in and out of bedrooms was nearly impossible with this layout.

"Come and get it. I have iced tea or a variety of fruit juices or even beer."

Dad tutted, and from the corner of my eye, I saw him shaking his head.

"I hope you're not seriously going to be plying my girl with drink. You know she's nineteen."

Ouch. That stung, and I'd bet Sophie didn't like it. No one wanted to be treated like a child when they'd become an adult in every sense of the word except not legally old enough for alcohol.

Barbara sounded stern, but her face displayed a soft expression; her eyes smiled. Perhaps she was joking; I couldn't be sure. And I didn't know my dad's new wife well enough to be sure of her sense of humor.

Before I could answer, Sophie had walked up alongside me, bringing her subtle perfume. Sweet, with a hint of strawberry, and a dash of deliciously distracting.

"I'm easy and twenty." She whispered the number quietly, and I expect only I heard it. "Tea, water, soda, they're all good for me."

I opened the fridge again; Sophie leaned in and picked up a can of soda. I pulled out tea for Barbara.

"Do you have any idea what your hours will be at college?" I asked.

"No. I'll get my schedule tomorrow. I'm planning to make the most of it, though. Go to every class and make the most of every opportunity."

I wondered if that were true or if she said that for the benefit of her mom.

"What kind of art are you doing?"

"Well, that's just it. I'm not sure. I love sketching and painting. Country scenes, still life, watercolors, oils. But it's a bit old-fashioned, so I'm not sure there's a demand. I think I should probably improve my photography skills and, well, I need to decide what I'm going to do when I grow up." She shrugged and looked around at her mom and my dad.

I sensed she might have different things to say if we were alone.

"You're welcome to try out my camera and play with my software. I'm not exactly a beginner when it comes to photo editing software. In fact, I think I might have every program available."

"I didn't know you were into photography." Sophie jerked her head back, and I was, in turn, taken aback by her surprise.

"Seriously, do you know anything about me?" I looked across at Dad, who paid us no attention while he discussed the view with Barbara. I interrupted. "Dad," I interrupted. "Have you told Sophie anything about us?"

"Yes," he said without glancing in our direction.

I shook my head and shrugged. "Does he even know me?" I whispered. "I've been taking photos and manipulating images for as long as I can remember. And I'm studying photography and business."

Sophie smiled. "How didn't I know that?"

"Right. How didn't you?" I shot laser beams at my dad with my eyeballs. Imaginary lasers, of course. "I'd show you my equipment right now, but it would be easiest if you just came into my bedroom to see it. And I'm not sure your mom would approve."

Her grin widened. "Definitely. Visits to each other's bedrooms are postponed until after they've gone. I'm pleased to find out I've got something in common with at least one of you. I've been apprehensive about suddenly moving in with a bunch of guys."

"I understand. It's like we've met a few times and made polite conversation, but we don't actually know each other. You'll find we're very easy going. You'll be fine."

"I'm sure that's true. So you're an artist. Wow."

For a moment, I just basked in her warm enthusiasm. "There's a photography exhibition at the Clinton Arts Center next week. We could go together. I'd love to hear what you think of it."

"What I think? Why? Do you know anyone who's exhibiting there?"

"I might happen to know someone."

CHAPTER THREE
SOPHIE

Laying his knife down on his almost empty plate, Ben looked at my mom and said, "You don't need to worry about Sophie. It's very safe around here." He swiped his fingers through the air a few times, adding emphasis to his statement before picking up his wine glass. "And I'll drive her everywhere."

Annoyingly, the men sitting either side of me at this round dinner table opted for red wine. It only drew further attention to the fact that I'm younger than them and too young to drink legally.

"I hope you will." Mom sighed and glanced at me before turning her attention back to Ben. "It'd set my mind at rest. I'm worried about her out on these city streets, especially at night after dark."

"Mom is convinced that would-be attackers hang out on street corners. And like vampires or zombies, they all come out at night," I said. I'd always be Mommy's little girl, especially while I was a teenager. Nevertheless, I was big enough and old enough to walk to and from my classes every day without anyone holding my hand.

Ben winked at me. He put the wine glass down on the white cotton tablecloth and focused all of his attention back on my mom, sitting on the other side of him. "Between Adam, Carl, and me, it will be as if she has a personal chauffeur and bodyguard. Twenty-four seven. You don't need to worry."

Annoyed by the way they spoke about me as if I wasn't even there, I stifled a disgruntled cough against my clenched fist. Sitting next to Ben at the table, I didn't know whether to voice my objection to the way they talked about me as if I were a child, or join in the other conversation at the dinner table.

To my left, Adam spoke with his dad. I caught snippets about a nightclub and dance music and Europe, but I didn't hear enough to join in.

When I looked in his direction, Carl smiled sweetly. Apparently, I'd caught him watching me from directly across the table.

My body heated inexplicably, and I was sure I blushed as I returned a smile. If anyone noticed my reddening cheeks, hopefully, they'd attribute it to the warm food.

I knew Mom would find Ben's words reassuring, believing I had an escort everywhere I went. Ben had picked up on her fears.

Rather than presume I'd appreciate a lift or a personal bodyguard, I'd have preferred it if Ben asked first. However, I realized that wasn't what the conversation was about. Not really.

It wasn't about looking after me and taking away my freedom to decide. This conversation was entirely about reassuring Mom of my safety. From her point of view, she was leaving her little girl, albeit her eldest daughter, to live alone in the big city.

Conscious of my mom's concerns, Ben was doing me a great favor, in a way, by putting her mind at ease.

I could do without her fussing and worrying. Calling me all the time to check on my safety and monitoring the Find My Daughter App on the phone to track my whereabouts.

"We generally take turns at cooking at home; that way, we can each look forward to three nights off. That's if Sophie wants to join in the schedule." Ben turned to focus on me.

And, upon hearing my name, I turned my attention toward him.

It seemed very intense looking into each other's eyes at such close quarters.

Ben's facial features were hardly discernible from Carl's.

Incredibly handsome across a table and almost irresistible when close enough to kiss.

It began to occur to me that living surrounded by three equally gorgeous identical triplets might become a problem. Men I rather liked.

In my limited experience, the Cooper brothers were easy to like. They were polite and considerate, as well as attractive and sexy. And they lived in a luxurious penthouse paid for by their rich father. My stepfather.

The triplets couldn't be completely perfect. I just didn't know them well enough to know their faults.

I decided then that for my sanity, I had to focus on finding some reasons not to like them so much because they could offer a lot of temptation.

I looked away again, a little too quickly.

"You don't have to decide now, Sophie, but it would be weird if we three cooked for each other and left you out."

Before I came up with a reply, my mom butted in, "Sophie's a reasonable cook, but what about you boys? Will she get a bad deal on the days you cook?" She raised an eyebrow, pursed her lips, and looked very skeptical.

"Hey, well said, Mom." I laughed. So did Mom and Ben.

Three dudes, the sons of wealthy parents, probably grew up with all of life's privileges. Of course, Mom would expect them not to cook.

"We don't live on takeout and frozen pizza every night, I'll have you know. Just once or twice a week when it's my turn to cook." Ben chuckled at his joke. "Adam's our star chef; he seems to enjoy planning meals, but Carl makes a reasonable effort too."

Hearing his name mentioned attracted Adam's attention.

"Who's talking about me, and what's he saying?" Sitting on the other side of me, Adam turned from the conversation with his father.

I turned to the sound of his voice, and it struck me how much I was sandwiched in between these guys, for better or worse, and all that meant.

In the apartment, my bedroom was between Adam's and Ben's; I'd basically be sleeping between the two of them with Carl's room located across the hall from mine. Effectively, we'd sleep in the same arrangement as how we sat at this table.

"Adam, Ben's been telling me that you boys will look after Sophie for me," Mom said.

Ben's arm snaked around my shoulder, and his warm breath floated close to my ear.

"Like our sister," Ben explained to Adam. "We'll take turns cooking for her and see her safely to and from school. Isn't that right, Adam."

My heart raced. I froze at the close contact and didn't know what to make of it. Enjoying the feeling in a way that I shouldn't, it created confused feelings. Not helped by the fact that there were three of them, and to me, they looked equally handsome.

I couldn't tell them apart.

Their dad knew the difference as soon as he saw them. At the apartment earlier, he knew it was Carl who opened the door. He could tell the difference between Adam and Ben when they arrived home. I had to work it out by listening to the conversation and remembering their identities according to their clothes.

I knew who was who at the table because they all wore different colored tops.

If they all went to the bathroom and swapped shirts, and then returned to sit in each other's seats, I'd not know about it.

Each day when they wear new clothes, I was going to have to work out who was who again, like those people I read about with amnesia. I'd be fine so long as they always wear different colored shirts from each other. If they ever swap shirts or wear the same clothes, I'd be lost.

Adam didn't seem to notice the fire in my eyes as I looked at him. He looked into my eyes very briefly and then said to my mother, "Most definitely we'll protect her. She's safe with us."

"That's reassuring because she's not used to the ways of the city. She'll need protection from men as she's got no experience. She's saving herself for the right man."

And that was when I died.

I didn't actually die, unfortunately.

Even though my cheeks flamed hot enough for spontaneous combustion, I continued to live and suffer the humiliation of all eyes on me as they realized what my mom had just said.

Ben withdrew his arm, and I turned my attention to my plate as the boys registered that I'd never had a boyfriend, at least, not that my mom knew about.

At almost twenty years of age, I was already older than many people who were leaving home to go to college for the first time. Family circumstances had set me back a year, what with Dad's death and our family finances prior to Mom's current marriage.

I didn't need everyone knowing I was a virgin too.

I'd taken heed of Mom's advice to save myself for someone special, and that such intimacy would be better with someone who loves me and cares for me.

But I didn't want everyone to know I'd never so much as had a boyfriend.

No one was a virgin past eighteen these days — no one except me.

I was old enough to know how uncool it sounded. It made me seem like a freak or loser — the sad girl who couldn't get a boyfriend. Life hadn't been like that for me.

Oh, God, Mom.

How embarrassing.

I never wanted to go out for this "family dinner."

TRIPLET TIME 19

I'd have liked Mom and Mr. Cooper to drop me and my stuff off at the apartment and leave me to get on with this new chapter of my life.

I can understand why they wanted a family meal, though.

The triplets had lived away from home for a while, and as their wealthy dad owned the apartment outright, they stayed there all year round. They didn't come home on vacation for weeks on end, just for the briefest overnight stay on holidays.

Theirs was a lovely apartment in the city, and we lived in a small town, so I understood why they'd rather stay here where they are grown up and independent.

The boys didn't miss the comment about my status. I could see a look in their eyes as they all registered my virginity.

CHAPTER FOUR
ADAM

"Sophie, are you coming?" I called after knocking on her bedroom door.

"That's a bit personal," Carl called from his bedroom.

"To breakfast," I sighed. "I swear I live with overgrown teenagers."

I knocked again and called out. "Do you want to come out for breakfast?"

She'd been enthusiastic about the plan when we talked about it at dinner yesterday.

It had been Carl's turn to put food on our plates, so we had something we could have invited hippy vegans to eat. Quinoa with fresh herbs, home chopped coleslaw, and tofu. *Tofu!*

None of us were even vegetarian. It tasted delicious, but I didn't tell Carl that. I didn't want to encourage his belief that such healthy, meat-free-fare was acceptable.

Ben and I picked up a burger later when we were out, but then we went to the nightclub, so we were out very late.

We'd gotten through two weeks of eating at home for our evening meals without a single takeout up until then. After dinner, some days we'd chat and watch TV together, although we'd all gone to our rooms early most nights to do more work or get ready for an early start in the morning.

I knocked again. "Breakfast at Bunny's. Our good old American, family-run greasy spoon."

"Remember it's the best breakfast this side of the river," Carl called out loudly from his bedroom opposite. His voice boomed through the open doorway.

"After feeding us rabbit food yesterday, I'm not sure his commendations are worth anything to a restaurant," Ben whispered as he sidled up beside me. He slouched against the wall by her door.

"And it's so close to our apartment we could just go down there in our slippers," he called out for Sophie to hear.

"Since when did slovenly footwear become a unique selling point?" I asked.

Raising just one shoulder, Ben shrugged and grinned.

"We'll wait for you if you're not ready," I added more loudly to the door.

"Hold on," she called out. Suddenly, the door opened. "I'm ready."

My eye level passed over her head; she was so much shorter than me. "Ready for what though?"

I lowered my gaze and found myself with a view of a cleavage that I hadn't prepared for. A lot of cleavage. Where had that come from?

I'd noticed her breasts before; of course, I would, I was a guy. But I didn't expect to see them so pleasantly presented for breakfast.

In the two weeks since she'd moved in, she'd kept them hidden under big, shapeless, sexless clothes. She dressed like a typical art student, genderless. I know it was a stereotype, so I wouldn't say it out loud, but it had crossed my mind that she might be a lesbian.

Of course, lesbians can dress like feminine hot babes too. And I was not going to admit to any fantasies or a porn collection involving large-breasted lesbians.

"Put your eyes back in your head, Adam." Ben gave me a friendly shove and brought additional attention to my inappropriate focus. Thanks, Bro.

Of course, he was just trying to make himself seem so much better than me.

Me the sexist pig, whereas he only saw the brilliance of her mind and personality. As if he wasn't captivated by the way the low cut, figure-hugging T-shirt beautifully displayed her character.

Did Sophie seem offended? No, thankfully, she giggled. I stepped back, allowing her to escape from her room.

Carl shot out from his bedroom and opened the front door.

We were all ready to leave.

"I'm excited about this trip out with you guys," she said as she threaded her arm through mine and we stepped toward the door, leaving my brothers to follow behind. "I wasn't sure if you might bail on me, though, as you were out late last night. I thought you might, you know, get lucky."

"Well, Ben usually goes home with a different girl every weekend, but his pick-up lines are getting old now." I flipped Ben the bird behind my back. "You should come out clubbing with us."

We didn't have to wait long for the elevator and soon we were on our way down. She looked tiny, standing in between us.

"I'd love to come clubbing." Her face lit up for a moment, and then the spark disappeared. "Would it be all right?"

"Yes. You'd be my guest. You'd come into the DJ booth, get free drinks, and dance with Ben."

No wonder he grinned like the cat who got the cream. I only realized after I'd said it, of course, I've just about paired them up. If Sophie came as my guest to the nightclub where I worked as a DJ, I'd be working as a DJ, and leaving her in Ben's safe hands.

And Ben was irresistible.

I know we looked almost alike, but that wasn't my ego talking.

It was based on what I saw. Women found Ben irresistible. It was a low move of mine to hint that he slept with more women than he cooked dinners. But it was true that they couldn't keep their eyes or their hands off him.

"I was thinking about my age," Sophie said.

"Oh, yes. You're not twenty-one yet. That hadn't occurred to me. As my guest, rather than a paying customer, it'll be no problem. No one'll ask your age."

She gave me a beaming smile, one to rival Ben's.

We reached the ground floor, the elevator doors opened, and we stepped out of the car.

She took Carl's arm, just as she'd taken mine. "Don't you want to go to the nightclub too?"

Ben and I fell in behind, and I heard Carl muttering something about it not being his thing. It wasn't as if he needed an excuse for a night out with Sophie. They'd spent the most time together since she arrived. Spending time in his room at his computer screens. Yes, multiple computers, multiple screens.

Hats off to the man, he did take some good photographs.

At last, in Sophie, he found someone he could talk to about photography. Someone who shared his interest and wanted to talk about it and look at photographs for hours on end.

Last weekend Carl and Sophie disappeared. Ben and I didn't see them. They toured art galleries for two days, apparently, and just slipped home to go to bed. Separate beds, I was sure of that.

It could have gone two ways. The addition of Sophie to the apartment could have changed everything for the better or the worse. We all knew things were going to change. The atmosphere in our apartment buzzed with life since Sophie moved in.

A change was inevitable, eventually.

Someday we would meet women, marry, and settle down. I couldn't envision it, though. We'd been together all our lives, and it was hard to imagine living apart. I certainly didn't think that'd be anytime soon.

Monday to Friday, she stayed at college for long hours. She couldn't have been in classes all that time. But she was an artist. They booked studio times. Went to the galleries. Sat in the parks sketching trees, flowers, and people.

I guessed she had been getting to know the city with her new college buddies. If she had any downtime in the day, she would be staying at college and hanging out with her classmates.

We had all been busy in the day with our respective college courses. Sophie could afford to take it easy at this stage, but she was over-enthusiastic, being in the first few weeks of her first year.

We three were in our final year, so the pressure was really on us.

We had pretty much had our evening meals and chilled at home each evening.

This breakfast was the first time we had all gone out together in the two weeks since we went out with our parents.

Bunny's was literally the very next building, and there was a walk of a few feet between our doors.

We entered the door, and I think all of our faces must have registered surprise and disappointment at not one single empty table. Of course, we'd left a little late, and everyone was out for breakfast. We all turned, looking every which way.

"We can wait for a table," I suggested.

At the same time, Carl said, "We can eat at home."

"Over there," Ben said, looking over my shoulder. I turned to see a family of two adults and two small kids in the highly coveted window booth, and it seemed they were preparing to leave. They were picking various items off the table, kid's books and toys, face cloths, hand sanitizer, and slipping them into bags. I loitered to stake a claim on these seats, not wanting to hurry the people on rudely.

"Hey, you can have this table." The lady saw our tableless plight.

"Thanks," I replied. "You take your time."

"We're ready to leave. We've already settled up. Sorry about the mess. The kids can't eat anything without throwing half of it on the table."

After a couple of minutes, we sat down at the freshly wiped table, and Sophie picked up the menu. The rest of us pretty much knew it by heart.

I couldn't complain about Carl sitting next to Sophie because I got to sit opposite her and the view from where I sat wasn't bad at all. And I didn't just mean out of the window.

Sophie held on to a menu. "This looks fabulous. I can't believe I haven't been here already."

"We could have done this last weekend." Ben cocked his head and looked sternly at Carl, who, in turn, looked back defiantly.

"Carl took me on a grand tour of art-related places. We went to The Athena Gallery, Clinton Arts Center, and a few other places where artists hang out and work."

"Did you go to the market along the river?" Ben asked. The weekly art market that ran alongside the river was one of our favorite places for a walk on Sunday morning when we first moved to the city, so I understood how Sophie felt about it. We didn't often go there together anymore.

Carl nodded. "Of course."

"Oh, yes. Where local artists have stands and hang their work along the fence? That was a nice event. I loved how it seemed like an open-air exhibition." Sophie oozed enthusiasm. "The variety and quality of work was amazing. We have to go again."

A part of me wished I'd been there with her too, sharing her enjoyment of it for her first time. No wonder Carl looked a little smug.

They must have had a great time together, and he had gotten a little closer to Sophie than Ben and I. In the playful competition between us for Sophie's affections, so far, Carl was well ahead.

"So you guys are really going to take me to the nightclub? What time will we leave? I wonder what I should wear. I don't think I've got anything appropriate."

I nodded and smiled at her excitement. She reminded me of a kid talking about Christmas.

"We'll go shopping when we leave here," said Ben.

Most girls love shopping. I couldn't help feeling both my brothers were making moves to build themselves up in her esteem. And feared I might be lagging behind.

"To be honest, I can't believe you're a DJ, Adam." She looked at me, and I didn't know what to say.

Ben saved me by asking what was on my mind. "Why do you say that? It'd be a strange thing to make up, and you'll see him at work when we go to the club."

"I'm not saying he's lying. But you three are not what you seem. You are so different to what I expected, and full of surprises."

"Surprises?" I asked. "What surprises?"

And judging by the confused expressions on my brother's faces, they were as mystified as me.

"Well, that you are a nightclub DJ, for one thing. It's not the sort of part-time job I'd imagine for a man getting a business degree. And you're from a wealthy family, so it's not as if you need the money from a part-time job." She bit her bottom lip, and a red flush climbed her neck. "I'm sorry."

What embarrassing thing was she thinking? "No, it's okay. But what else?" I asked. "You looked as if there was more to say."

"Well, you're all so good looking that I felt sure you'd have girlfriends or a stream of women visiting and stopping over."

Before we responded, she rushed on.

"And then you're all studying some kind of business degrees, which sound really boring." She looked around, and none of us denied it. "But it turns out you guys aren't the stuffy business-suit types. It's like you are hiding different people under your shirts."

Ben stood up. "I'll show you what I'm hiding under my shirt," he said as he raised his top to reveal a few inches of his toned, washboard abs. Any excuse to show his six-pack.

Sophie's eyes almost popped out of her head.

"Put it away, Ben. You'll put us off our food," I snapped. He might be less inclined to do that after he'd tucked into the huge plate that he'd ordered.

He grinned and sat back down. He was showing off for Sophie's benefit, and she seemed to lap it up.

"I didn't mean that," said Sophie. "I meant, on the face of it, you three are doing what's expected; you are all doing a sensible business degree. Even if it is combined with photography." We all looked at Carl.

He tapped his forehead.

"So you can take up sensible business careers like your father expects," Sophie continued. "But underneath the straight-laced facade, you all seem artistic. Carl, with his photography. You with your music and cooking, Adam. The two of you are so creative. As for Ben, well, I'm not sure what exactly, but I think I'm going to discover you write poetry or something."

"Oh, no," Carl mumbled, shaking his head. "Cue a poem."

As I would have predicted, Ben launched into an overly dramatic recitation:

"Yet if hope has flown away
In a night, or in a day,
In a vision, or in none,
Is it therefore the less gone?
All that we see or seem
Is but a dream within a dream."

Carl and I rolled our eyes and made tortured groaning sounds.

With luck, he would end there.

Sophie giggled and clapped when he paused. "What was that? Did you write it?"

"No. I had to learn some Edgar Allen Poe a few years ago and haven't been able to forget it. No, I'm not a poet. I just like to practice the art of love."

"Stop." I put my hands up to signal my surrender, and Carl placed his hands on his ears.

Sophie giggled some more. Either she was being polite or found him more amusing than we did.

Ben shrugged. "Okay, I'll admit my artistic skills are limited to martial arts."

Carl rolled his eyes.

"Oh, yes. Tae kwon do, I hadn't thought of that as an art," said Sophie.

"One day, I'll show you my moves." It seemed Ben really had perfected the art of corny lines to woo women. "My best moves are on the dance floor, of course. These hips were made for dancing."

"You're so funny." She giggled again. "Why don't you come to the nightclub with us, Carl? It'll be fun."

Carl looked across diagonally across the table at me for a moment.

Triplets did not share one brain or communicate telepathically despite what some would suggest. Nevertheless, having lived in close proximity for over twenty years, sometimes we sort of knew what each other was thinking.

At that precise moment, I felt certain all three of us knew, when it came to Sophie, it was game on. Her stepsister status wasn't going to deter any one of us. We all liked her too much.

And if we didn't, then she'd date some other guy.

Why should we watch her date other men without being in with a chance ourselves?

Sophie was too good a woman to let her slip by the three of us.

Slowly, Carl shook his head. "Um. It's not my scene. The three of us might look the same, but underneath the three very similar handsome dashing exteriors, we are quite different." He waved a hand across the table. "Those two got the musical and dancing talents along with the capacity to stay awake after midnight."

"Carl doesn't like nightclubs, loud music, or any music composed after 1950," Ben explained.

We all laughed. Ben was right.

"Oh, yes, we went to a jazz cafe last week for lunch. I didn't think about it at the time. Is that your kind of music?"

Carl nodded. "Jazz, among other things."

"Oh, I like that cafe, the Clinton Jazz Cafe," said Ben. "To be fair, they do play some good music. And they have live bands quite often."

CHAPTER FIVE
SOPHIE

By many people's standards, we arrived at the nightclub very early in the evening. Nevertheless, there was a small crowd of people gathered near the door. I assume they intended to go in and were perhaps waiting for additional friends to turn up.

The doors were open, and we heard the thumping bass from the sidewalk.

Like giant bodyguards, Adam and Ben were on either side of me as we approached the gray building.

"If you're the first DJ of the evening, who's playing the music now?" I asked Adam to my right.

"At this time of night, the club is practically empty, and nobody dances, so they just play a pre-recorded mix. They figure there's no point paying a DJ to stand in a booth when the club is just opening, and there are no customers," he replied.

Ben placed an arm around my shoulder, pulling me closer to him. "You'll see. There might be ten people in here right now, but it will fill up quickly over the next hour."

He must've sensed my apprehension, and he kept his arm around me as we approached the door.

Despite Adam's earlier assurances, I remained concerned that I might not be allowed in. It would be embarrassing, and I'd have to make my way back home alone. I couldn't expect Ben to come with me. He'd already hung out with me all day.

I feared that when we got to the door, someone would want to check my ID, but we sauntered past the short line and entered without a second glance from the security guys.

It turned out, Adam was correct. He should know what he was talking about as he did one or two DJ sets at this nightclub each week.

The inexperienced and naive small-town girl that I am, I'd never been to such a venue.

Fake ID was easy enough to come by, so I heard; that wasn't the issue. A lack of opportunity had been the problem. There simply wasn't a nightclub for miles in any direction near the small town in which I'd grown up. The nearest nightclub was in the city, which was simply too far away.

Just inside, Adam approached the lady at the register and spoke with her while I hung back with Ben. I could smell him, faintly. His cologne smelled nice. His arm around me made me feel looked after and wanted. I knew it was a brotherly arm, just as he might place it around the shoulders of a male friend or one of his actual brothers.

The three of us went through a second set of doors where stairs descended toward the sound of the music.

Inside the club, the bright spotlights revealed a cavernous, almost empty, space. I found it difficult to reconcile with my image of a nightclub full of dancing sweaty people. As it was, I saw dark silhouettes moving around the edge of the room. There were a few people there, but not many.

"You won't recognize this place within an hour, it will flood with people," Ben whispered in my ear.

I wondered if I'd run into anyone from my course. The thought lasted a moment before I remembered, like me, most of the classmates were too young to get in.

Adam led the way across the club, and Ben let his arm drop from my shoulder. When we reached the other side of the room, Adam tapped a keypad code and opened a door marked private. To be honest, the door was black, and I suspected most people wouldn't notice it there.

We entered the staff area.

The dark space was the size of a cupboard; it turned out to be an Antechamber. In contrast, the room beyond was brightly lit, and the sound of the nightclub merely a muffled background noise. When my eyes adjusted to the bright light, I realized this wasn't just one room; I saw open doors suggesting a suite of rooms.

"Welcome to the very unglamorous staff area where people come to take a break." Adam spread out his arms and turned around.

It reminded me of a waiting room with uncomfortable chairs and a grubby carpet. Not a place you'd want to stay and relax in for any longer than necessary. "There are lockers through here." He led the way into the next room, and I followed. Like a gentleman, Ben hung back, waiting for me to go first.

There were indeed many lockers, some of them locked, others left open with keys in the doors.

"If you want to leave your stuff in here, your jacket or anything, this is the place to put it. Of course, you can use the club coat check, it's only a few dollars, but there's always a long line."

Adam pulled a key out of his pocket. "I left my equipment here yesterday." He opened a locker door and pulled out a headset. "Apart from getting this, I don't need to come here because I'm just doing one set, then I'm finished for the night. And everything I need is here." He pulled a memory stick out of his pocket.

I had no idea what being a nightclub DJ involved, but I was quickly getting the idea. "Do you leave your headset here all week?" I knew he only did one or at most two nights a week, and always the first shift.

"Not usually, no, just sometimes overnight." Adam fished his free hand into his other pocket and pulled out a pile of coins. At least I thought they were coins. He handed them all over to Ben. "Next stop the bar and then the DJ booth."

"Drink tokens," Ben replied to my questioning expression without any further explanation. "Okay, let's go. Um, first, I'm going to leave my sweater here. Do you want to put your jacket in a locker too?"

I did. We shared a locker. Adam slipped the key into his pocket.

It seems they didn't trust me with much. Or they were looking after me like older brothers. I could choose which way I wanted to interpret their actions.

We must have only been in the staff room for five or ten minutes, but when we came out, the club was already noticeably busier.

The three of us made our way slowly to the bar.

Slowly, because everyone wanted to stop and talk to Adam and Ben as if they were celebrities in this place.

Adam worked there, giving everyone a good time, so I understood why people all wanted to speak to him. Ben, however? Perhaps it was because they looked alike?

I'd gotten the hang of telling them apart when I saw them every day. I guess there, in the dark of the club, most people probably couldn't tell who was who, so they showed a flattering interest in both of them.

A part of me was thrilled that my roommates and stepbrothers were so popular.

Another part of me felt protective of them. Well, jealous, if I was honest. I didn't want to share the brothers with their admirers. I wanted to keep them for myself.

And many of these people were admirers. I could tell by the way both men and women looked over the hot bodies of my two men. I hadn't found out if they were gay or straight yet. Perhaps the fact that they hadn't responded to my comment about having a stream of girlfriends meant they were gay. All three of them? They hadn't had a stream of boyfriends back to the apartment either.

When we finally reached the bar, Ben asked me if I'd like a bottle of water. Water? He must have seen the surprise on my face because before I questioned his sanity, he explained that they both drank water when they were here. Well, if it was good enough for my older brothers, then I didn't mind doing the same.

"Right, I'm taking off to the DJ booth. You two come up and see me when you're ready," Adam said when Ben handed him a bottle of water.

"Will do," I said and watched him walk away. Again stopped by everyone in his path, I wondered how long it would take before he got there.

"Why water and not something more exciting?" I asked Ben when he passed me my bottle and stepped away from the bar.

He reacted with a tentative smile. It couldn't have been a strange question, but he took a while to answer. Finally, he said, "It's healthy; it's kind on your teeth; how many reasons do you want?"

At each comment, my eyebrows raise a little higher as if they had a mind of their own. "One good reason would do."

He held up his hand with his fingers spread. "No calories. No hangover. Good for hydration when dancing." And he counted them off. "There are three reasons straight off."

I felt a little childish as if I'd assumed that alcohol became a compulsory part of a night out for people over twenty-one.

"We might come out at night, but we don't stay out all night. We go home at a fairly reasonable time, and by drinking water, we can get up and function the next day."

"We. We. We."

"Yes. Me and Adam. Although Carl's much the same. He doesn't drink much either. We haven't got the time to spare to lose it to a hangover."

"I meant you always talk about yourselves, you and your brothers, as a group. You say we a lot when other people might say I or me." They all said, it a lot. I couldn't imagine many brothers in their twenties living together by choice and being as close as the triplets.

"I do? Or do we?"

"All this talking about wee and drinking. I've got to go use the ladies' room."

"Oh, right." Ben laughed. "I'll come with you. Not like, um, completely come with you into the bathroom. But I'll show you where they are and hold your drink."

Just as well, we set off in plenty of time as it turned out, the bathrooms were not handy. We had to go out of the bar and up some stairs and along a corridor. It seemed as if we were trekking to a different building. And all the way, people stopped to talk to Ben.

Not just people.

Specifically women.

Women with flirting smiles, and roving eyes, and roaming touches.

And he smiled back.

Jealousy flared within me because I wanted to keep his flirty attention to myself.

I'd gotten so comfortable with the triplets that I wasn't nervous around them any longer. It was as comfortable as if we'd been friends for years.

After living with them for a while, I could tell the guys apart at a glance, but I still found each of them attractive, each in his own way. Much as I tried to bury it, I had to admit that I fancied each one of them like crazy, and I wouldn't want to choose between them. When Ben bared his stomach in the diner, I practically purred. I imagined running my fingers over it and stroking that thick treasure trail that ran central and downward into his pants.

The attraction wasn't only because they looked like calendar models. They each had very different personalities, but all of them were kind, considerate, and gentle.

Although the huge space was by no means full and not even halfway there, I was beginning to understand what Ben meant when he said it would flood with people. Nightclub goers seemed to be pouring in. Every few minutes, the cavernous club looked less and less empty.

By the time my visit to the bathroom was done, I was certain Adam had started his musical stint. There was a different vibe in the air, and many people were dancing.

We stood, hovering near a table, at the edge of the dance floor.

Ben slipped his arm around my shoulder again and whispered in my ear, "Let me know when you want to get out there and dance."

I looked up at him. "Are you itching to dance?"

His whole body seemed to be tapping along with the rhythm, and he enviously watched the people moving.

He looked down at me and nodded. "I love this music. Don't you?"

Nodding, I felt like one of the children seduced by the Pied Piper of Hamelin. With the loud volume of the music, the way the base rhythm pulsed through my bones, or the way Adam mixed one track seamlessly into the next, I was eager to dance too. I had to admit, I did love it.

Other people's enthusiasm was also infectious. Everyone looked like they were having fun.

Ben finished off his water, so I did the same, and we went out onto the dance floor.

Joyfully, with smiles on our faces and our arms in the air, we moved with the beat. We made the most of the space, and as people crowded in around us, we moved closer together. Ben was a great dancer. His eyes and his hands were all over me in a way that felt good and respectful. We had fun. I held his attention, and he held mine.

At times we held hands. We placed our hands on each other's bodies. His on my hips and mine on his shoulders and his arms. I got hotter when I touched his muscular arms.

Sometimes, when we weren't physically touching, we connected in other ways. Mimicking each other's moves, our eyes fixed upon each other.

My heart beat fast and faster, and it wasn't just from the physical activity.

When I turned my back to him, his arm slipped around my waist; his hand lay flat against my stomach, and we closed the distance until his groin rubbed against my ass.

It felt sexy moving to the music with Ben in that way, exactly the way other people danced too.

It was innocent and fun until something snapped.

Heat and desire pulsed through me in time with the music.

Temptation mere inches away from me and dancing at the end of my fingertips: my stepbrother. Me, sandwiched between Ben, who was physically on the dance floor with me, and Adam in spirit, playing the fantastic music.

When another club favorite came on, my hands flew in the air along with everyone else's except Ben's; they wrapped around my waist as he moved into my personal space until he couldn't get any closer.

Not unless we removed clothes.

The lower part of our bodies sealed together, grinding. A seal that moved higher and higher. My chest against his toned torso, his groin against my waist.

He stooped, allowing his mouth to find mine open and relaxed for the first perfect kiss. His mouth tasted of hot goodness and temptation. I wasn't entirely sure whether he instigated this or I did. It wasn't that he kissed me or I kissed him. We just both seem drawn to each other.

Melting in his arms, it sounded like such a cliche, but that was how it went.

Touching his arms, my hands worked up over his toned muscles. I could only feel my desire getting stronger. Even my most conscious thoughts were that I wanted this to go so much further. And I couldn't understand why I had been fighting to keep the brothers at arm's length.

We continued to kiss, and a pang of guilt hit me.

I'd thought of his brothers.

Even while I kissed Ben, I'd thought about how I'd like to kiss his brothers.

They were three very different people, and yet, my innermost thoughts treated them as if they were interchangeable when it came to attraction.

I knew it must be wrong to think about different men when kissing a guy, and if he knew, he wouldn't like it. It must be even worse to think about that guy's brothers.

Still, I didn't stop kissing. It felt too good. Instead, I tried to block Adam and Carl from my mind.

After trying hard to ignore and deny the physical attraction that existed between each one of those triplet brothers and me, opportunity rather than conscious choice had guided Ben into my arms. I'd have reacted the same way to anyone one of the guys, and I didn't like that thought. I certainly wouldn't want to have to choose between them.

I wasn't sure where this was going to go, and a big part of me thought I should stop it, but I couldn't because I didn't want to. I wanted Ben badly.

CHAPTER SIX
BEN

I never thought I'd kiss my stepsister. And when they found out, my brothers wouldn't believe that it wasn't planned.

Sure, I flirted with her. I flirted with all women. I was friendly, it was just the way I was.

On the dance floor, she looked sexy, and I felt horny. I thought she liked me like that, and I definitely wanted her like that.

So we kissed, at last.

My brothers will never believe we kissed by accident. They might think I want Sophie as another notch on my bedpost. They already call me a Casanova who can't keep my hands to myself. An unjustified claim. It wasn't my fault; I was desirable and in demand.

Since Sophie moved into our home and I'd gotten to know her, with each passing day, I'd grown to like her more. I liked her self-confidence and independence.

I walk her to school each day, and we walk home together as well sometimes. It was no chore to me as I enjoyed getting the exercise and spending that time alone with Sophie. She didn't need me; she wasn't timid or frightened, but I had made a promise to her mother.

The problem was, the better I got to know her, the more I liked her. She was a lovely person and a member of our family.

So far, I had put my desire for her at the back of my mind, but it was there. I couldn't dream of bringing another woman back to our apartment, not now, not knowing Sophie was there sleeping in the room next to mine. No matter who came home with me, I'd prefer to be with Sophie. I couldn't be so disrespectful to sleep with a woman thinking of her as second best to the one I really wanted.

I'd managed to keep my attraction to Sophie guarded, but I lost control when my inhibitions were under the influence of the club atmosphere. Although, I wasn't sure it was entirely down to me. I didn't force myself on her. She seemed to be giving out come-get-me signals, and my body responded.

God, did my body respond.

My dick got so hard as we kissed. She must have felt it when we pressed closely against each other. I hoped she felt the same way. I wanted to take her home. If I were with another woman, that would have been an option, but with Sophie, I had a quandary or two.

It was her home too. She was my stepsister, and sleeping with her would have lasting consequences because of the family ties. You didn't have a one-night stand with someone in your close family, so I had to be sure it was more than that.

Nothing inside me wanted a one-night stand with Sophie. I wanted more. I'd never felt this way about a woman before. I knew she liked me too; however, I wasn't sure how she felt about "us."

My hand scrunched into the soft hair at the back of her head, and with my other, I caressed the soft skin of her cheek. The kiss lasted long enough for me to run my hands down her back and clench onto her cinched waist. My tongue explored the inside of her mouth and entwined with hers.

She had to feel as I did. Just as hot and full of desire.

I wanted to give her everything. To take home and show her a great time. To make her come while she lay on my bed calling my name.

My mind and heart filled with a mix of emotions, the like of which I had not previously experienced. Not merely familiar lust and desire, I'd had those before. There was something about Sophie I liked. Loved, if I was honest.

It was probably too early to say that word, but I loved everything about Sophie, and you get to know someone fairly well when you live with them as family, ate meals with them, and walked them to college every morning. We'd walked home together plenty of times too.

We kissed, and moved to the music, and held each other on the dance floor.

I enjoyed the moment and tried not to worry about what would happen next because I honestly had no idea where this would go.

There was a strong caveman urge inside me to take her like I wanted, with her permission, of course.

And then there were my brothers.

We'd talked about Sophie. Often, and in detail.

They both liked her from the start, just as I did. To look at, she was a cute chick. Before we got to know her, we all joked about how we wouldn't kick her out of bed. As we had gotten to know her, we didn't joke in the same way.

They liked her as a person as much as I did.

She was funny, caring, great company and gorgeous to look at. She was thoughtful and considerate, mature and independent. Her mom believed she needed looking after, but really, she didn't.

Kissing, we stayed on the dance floor for way too long and licked each other until we were dehydrated.

"Let's go get a drink," I whispered in her ear.

The first words that passed between us since we began kissing and touching in a way that siblings shouldn't.

She nodded.

We walked off the dance floor toward the bar.

Digging my hand into my pocket, I pulled out two tokens. If we were going to leave, we'd left our stuff in the locker, and although I knew the key number for the staffroom, Adam had the physical key for the locker. Even if I had the key, we'd have to tell him if we were leaving without him.

I asked for two bottles of water at the bar and handed over the drink tokens.

Sophie took one bottle, and I stared at the cap on my drink while considering my options. What next?

I took her hand and kissed her on the cheek. She had to understand; I didn't want what happened on the dance floor to stay on the dance floor. I wanted it to continue.

I moved my lips to her ear. "Do you want to get out of here? Your place or mine?"

She laughed and nodded.

There was chemistry between us. She experienced it too.

TRIPLET TIME

"Come on." I took her hand. We'd have to face Adam first.

We walked up to the DJ booth. He saw us through the door and opened it to let us in. He noticed the handholding straight away, and his gaze lingered on our entwined fingers, and his eyes widened with realization.

Numerous times over the years, people have told us that twins and triplets have their own language and communicate with telepathy.

Nonsense.

There are times when words aren't necessary if you know someone well enough, you've lived with them all of your life, and you've talked with them often. We didn't need to explain our intentions.

He didn't offer Sophie a tour of the booth. He was usually enthusiastic to show-off the equipment, but not this time. The lighting deck was particularly interesting, in my opinion. But Adam kept it set to automatic when in the booth on his own. He said thinking about the music was enough work for him. Later in the evening, a guy would turn up who had the sole job of running the light show.

Adam pulled out the locker key and gave it to me. "I'll see you at home tomorrow."

I nodded. "See you in the morning, bro."

Sophie and I walked back through the club to the staff area. Three people sat eating sandwiches and looking at the screens on their phones, unlike earlier, when we were the only people there. It really was a dreary staffroom.

It didn't seem the right place for a private conversation, so we retrieved our items from the locker in silence.

As we neared the doors to the exit of the nightclub, I stopped walking and stepped in front of Sophie. "Are you sure you're ready to leave? We can stay." Then, I brushed my lips over hers and licked her top lip with my tongue to reassure her of my intentions. Not wanting to influence her in any way, of course.

Her tongue came out to greet mine, and she stepped closer so that once again, our bodies pressed together, and a barely controllable desire grew within me. She answered only with actions.

I stepped back. "Keep that thought in mind. We'll be home soon."

Outside the club, we jumped in a cab. We continued to hold hands and didn't speak the whole way home, a journey that took about ten minutes.

In the elevator, we gazed into each other's eyes. It was time to tell her what I held inside. "I've wanted to kiss you like that for weeks since you moved in."

"I know," she replied. "I've seen the way you look at me."

"I like you, Sophie. You're special." Damn it. The words seemed so inadequate to express how I actually felt. I couldn't tell her all the things going on inside me.

She seemed calm about the whole thing.

If she was going to choose one of us out of my brothers and me, I thought I'd be the last on the list.

She spent the most time with Carl; they had their photography and art in common.

Adam charmed everyone with his fantastic cooking, and he behaved like a grown-up, living up to his status as the eldest.

I wasn't sure what she saw in me, but I was there, and they weren't.

Once I'd opened the apartment door, taking her hand, I led her into my bedroom at the furthest end of the hall, next to the living room.

Her room was next to Adam's; of course, he was still out. Carl was probably asleep across the hall.

We entered my bedroom. I shut the door behind us and turned on a lamp. She sat down on the edge of my bed and started to unlace her boots as if she'd done this many times before. I did the same, kicking them clear in a moment and then sat down beside her.

We kissed again. I didn't want my mouth to leave her.

My hands roamed freely over her body this time, not only over the top of her clothes, but skirting around the edges. I tucked my fingers inside her neckline, under her sleeves, eventually pulling her top up and over her head.

Her soft skin felt smooth and delicate under my touch.

She ran her hands over my body, the light touch sending electrical sparks scooting across my skin.

I unhooked her bra and eased her back so that she lay down in the middle of my bed. I kissed her neck while stroking her arms. She writhed under my touch.

We threaded our fingers together, and I pinned her hands on either side of her. She moaned and whimpered as I kissed, crossing her clavicle down to her soft breasts.

I licked around the curving mounds, one then the other. Finally, I moved to a nipple, which I teased with my tongue and gently nibbled with my teeth.

She squirmed and moaned a little louder and harder, indicating that she enjoyed every moment of my ministrations.

"Ben," she moaned. "Oh, Ben."

New music for my ears. Each sound. Each movement. They urged me on. I wanted to both be in her already and to take my time.

My cock was uncomfortably hard in my pants, but I had other stuff to focus on.

To make our first time together special.

I wanted her always to remember it and want to come back to me for more.

In the back of my mind, I also wondered how much experience she'd had. I recall her mom suggesting Sophie had no experience at all. It hadn't been confirmed or denied, but Sophie never spoke about any guys in her past.

It was possible Sophie was a virgin.

All the more pressure on me to make sure this was excellent for her. Not that I needed to fuck her to make her feel good. I had other skills that would definitely get her coming over and over with my name on her lips.

I thought we shouldn't go all the way only a short while after our first kiss. Not without discussing what it meant. I didn't want her to regret having sex with me because we were both swept away with lust.

I knew I wanted more than sex with her; I wanted a relationship.

If we were going to have sex, I wanted it to be a decision she'd thought about.

I let go of her hands and moved my hands down over her stomach and across her hips.

She squirmed and giggled.

"I found somewhere ticklish?" I asked.

"Just a little," she replied.

I tucked my hands into the top of her skirt.

"Hold on; there's a zipper." Twisting the skirt about her waist, she hurried to undo it.

With the skirt undone, I tugged it down then reached for her panties to follow.

CHAPTER SEVEN
SOPHIE

When he pulled my panties down, I felt a little embarrassed. If he noticed, what would he think about them being sopping wet? He must've seen; he politely didn't comment.

Naked, vulnerable, and incredibly turned on. That was me lying on my stepbrother's bed.

I'd never been naked like this, in front of a man, and so desperate for him to touch me. I wanted him to explore where I'd only ever touched myself.

Ben was still fully clothed except for his footwear, and I was lying naked on his bed. It was like a scene from one of my hottest and most secret fantasies: the one that involved the dominant muscular warrior taking the virgin slave girl when his gang of outlaws raided the medieval village. We all had fantasies like that, didn't we?

Yet, I was too shy to ask him to do certain things. Under the circumstances, I knew it sounded crazy, but I was shy. My excuse was that it was my first time.

I'd never been so aroused. The lead up to this situation seemed to have lasted forever. An hour or two, at least if it started in the nightclub. Or the days and weeks that I'd lived here. Every day Ben walked with me to school, and most days, he walked me home. In retrospect, it all seemed like flirting.

I shivered as his fingers passed over, making contact with my sensitive clit, and slipped between the swollen slippery wet folds of skin. He felt his way as if the route was familiar, and all the time, his gaze remained on my face.

Our eyes locked together as if engaged in an intense staring competition.

"You're so wet." His voice was gravelly deep with arousal.

Having him acknowledge what was happening to me only heightened the erotic experience. I felt dirty and rude. And I wanted to hear more of his comments.

A finger slipped inside me. Easily. I was so aroused.

He hummed his approval, and I gasped.

My chest rose and fell rapidly with my quickening breath. And I became conscious of my breathing. It partly distracted me from the full magnitude of what was happening lower down my body.

His fingers and palm touched me where no man had been before, bringing new sensations that were so unimaginably different to when I touched myself.

I gasped again in anticipation when Ben broke our eye contact, and he lowered his head down to where his fingers were so diligently working. When his warm wet tongue made contact, I near exploded.

He proceeded to lick around every sensitive inch but avoided direct contact with my clit. His tongue dipped between my damp folds of skin and ran along them.

Did he intend to make me beg? Because I was that close to doing any damn thing he wanted.

Teasing.

He proved an expert at teasing.

Just as he remained dressed, right then, when I wanted him naked.

I wanted to see Ben's dick, to touch it and feel it inside me. I wanted him to take me and take my virginity. Complete my transformation to womanhood. I wanted it all and in every position.

Who'd have thought I'd never done this before?

But the temptation and waiting had gone on for so long.

Even though at that moment, I had trouble remembering to breathe, I suddenly remembered I was a woman with free, independent will, and I could speak. "Can you take your clothes off, too, please?"

His tongue left my skin for a moment. He looked up at me with a grin. "I'm a little busy right now. Hands full, you know. I'll take them off in a moment."

I did know.

Ben licked and sucked my tender bud, and his unrelenting fingers worked magic inside me. Entering, curling, twisting.

Finger fucking me until what? When would this stop?

How was I going to survive this sexy onslaught? I thought he was going to make me come. While my stepbrother was fully clothed, I was so close to an orgasm. The thought of writhing naked under his mouth and fingers and coming in front of him. On his bed. Him still dressed. That was one dirty thought too much.

Heat rushed through my body, and I crashed over the precipice, no longer able to hold it together.

The most incredible orgasm of my life unleashed, and I couldn't stop it if I'd wanted to. The first one ever with someone else.

I couldn't think clearly.

My stepbrother's fingers inside me.

His tongue. On. My. Clit.

My naked body, writhing on his bed.

My orgasm. Gushing.

As the intensity of the moment subsided just a little, I felt full of such strong but confusing emotions, I didn't know whether I wanted to laugh or cry.

I'd come, but I wanted more.

This felt like a mere stepping stone to a new level of arousal.

All at once, his mouth was on mine, and he pulled me onto my side so that we could lay facing each other side-by-side. I wrapped my legs around him; my juices were undoubtedly and embarrassingly coating his pants. I wanted to rub against him. Rub, against his thigh and his bulging crotch. Discover his cock, and have it slide inside me.

I wanted it all.

And I had no idea I could feel like this.

The night couldn't be better.

It was perfect.

Okay.

The only thing that would've made it even better was if the other brothers were here, too.

Whoa!

That was so wrong.

Stop thinking about the other brothers.

Instead, I focused on the here and now. I could feel the outline of his hard cock in his pants, pressing against me.

"Can you take your clothes off now, please?" I asked.

He must have wanted to.

Letting go of me, Ben sprang off the bed and stood up. In a flash, he had his top off, then his pants and underwear swept down in one movement. His hard cock sprang free with a bounce.

This huge man was all in proportion.

When I saw the size of it, I had a moment of doubt. I wondered if I know what to do with it and whether, with my lack of experience, I'd be able to satisfy him.

At the same time, I was thrilled to think I'd done that to him. He was so hard. His cock was jutting out from his body and pointing at me.

When I saw the glistening wetness at the end, I wanted to taste it.

Without thinking about it, I sat up and moved quickly to kiss his cock while he was still standing by the bed.

In my mind, I wanted to take the whole thing into my mouth.

In reality, his cock was huge, and I doubted any human mouth could open that wide without a dislocated jaw. Instead, I licked around the end. The pleasant taste of his precum surprised me. And I licked up and down the shaft hoping my eager enthusiasm would compensate for my lack of experience.

And I loved the way he moaned.

He didn't seem to mind, or laugh at me, or asked me to stop. So it must've been okay.

And I didn't want to stop. It seemed an exciting thing to do and tasted far nicer than I'd ever imagined. Although when I opened my mouth wide to accommodate it, I could only take in the bulbous end. So I wrapped my hands around his thick shaft to investigate it with my fingers.

His thick hairy thighs were slightly apart, so I slipped one hand down to feel his balls, which elicited more encouraging moans as he muttered words that I couldn't make out.

After several minutes, Ben pulled away from me and got on the bed alongside me.

"You look so beautiful," he said as he brushed my hair back from my face.

Considering he was so much taller than me when we stood up when we laid next to each other, the height difference didn't seem so important. His arms were so long that he easily reached between my legs. When he touched me there again, my ability to think and act became seriously hindered.

"I love the way you react," he said.

I simply wanted to spread my legs, lay on my back, and let him do more of the same to me and anything else he wanted.

Anything at all.

I never realized sex would feel so good or how much I'd been missing by protecting my purity.

He lay beside me, and we kissed.

Without words, his kisses seemed to talk to me.

It may have been my imagination, but I felt wanted and desired.

I may have been confused by the fingers touching me, turning me on, and keeping me at a plateau of heightened arousal. I remained in a state of ecstasy between one orgasm and another.

Slipping my hand between us, I wrapped it around his hard dick and stroked up and down. He moaned into my mouth, and we kept kissing. Or at least licking tongues.

I wanted this feeling to last all night and forever. I couldn't think about what might happen after it ended and after we woke up from sleep or what the next day would bring.

I lived entirely in this glorious moment.

After some time, I suspected he was close to the edge too. His breathing became more ragged, and his body tensed. He pushed me onto my back and climbed on top of me briefly. His whole body covered mine, and he rutted against me. His cock slid back and forth against me for just a few brief seconds before he moved down the bed and between my legs.

"You taste so good, Sophie. I can't resist," he explained before his mouth sought out and made the connection with my most private area, yet again.

I submitted willingly.

And with his mouth and tongue and fingers thrilling me, I soon came again and again. Calling out loudly as I did so. "Ben! Ben! Oh, yes. Don't stop." I thrashed about upon his bed, out of control and not caring who heard me.

Adam wasn't home yet, Carl was across the hallway and asleep, but I couldn't bring myself to care. I was lost in ecstasy.

I expected Ben to fill me any moment.

Somehow he was astride me; his hand moved rapidly over his hard cock.

It was my own private show. I certainly found it thrilling to watch, and more so when white ribbons of cream spurted across my stomach.

For a few seconds, Ben stayed still, and the realization of what just happened sank in.

I'd just shared some very intimate times with my stepbrother.

We weren't even dating. And previously, I'd been saving myself for the right man.

Already, I'd thought about other men while I was with him, and not just once. I should've wanted only him, whereas I'd have been happy to do this with any one of three guys in my life. The three I happened to live with.

Without speaking, Ben got off me. Perhaps he was disgusted by my behavior. I wondered if, without realizing it, I'd spoken out loud about his brothers. But he quickly returned from the bathroom with a hand towel, which was slightly dampened in one corner. He cleaned my body tenderly, wiping any and all traces of his semen and my moment of doubt.

He showed me that he cared, and yet again, I felt looked after.

Each one of these brothers is too good for me.

"I hope you don't mind. You look so sexy, and I was so turned on."

"Mind? Why should I mind? That was great."

I was still riding the wave of ecstatic, erotic euphoria.

He threw the towel on the floor. As he slipped back into bed beside me, he wrapped his arms around me. I snuggled up to him and discovered resting my head on his expansive chest was extremely comfortable.

"Sophie, that was just the best, and you must know how I feel about you. You're amazing." His deep voice fell over me like a warm comfy blanket. Slowly he added, "I don't want you to think that you're just another girl to me. You're not; you're very special."

I didn't know where to begin to tell him how amazing it felt to me. I'd never done any of this stuff with a guy before, and I was embarrassed about my lack of experience.

What it would mean if the guy was so turned on by me as Ben appeared to be? It was thrilling to know that a man was so turned on by me that he came over me instead of waiting to come in me.

My eyes closed, and tiredness caught up with me all. "You too, Ben. You're very special too."

I lay there and thought I'd never sleep.

The next thing I knew, I was waking up, and many hours must've passed.

Somehow we'd come apart. My head was on the pillow instead of his chest. But his arms were still around me, and he held me close.

Being held in his arms felt so heavenly.

Even as he slept, I still felt wanted and loved and cherished. I so wanted to stay there forever.

Instead of drifting back to sleep, I lay awake.

My mind raced over the enormity of what had happened.

My mother had always told me to save myself for the right man, and it would be special when I met him.

Last night felt very special with Ben; the experience was something I couldn't believe I'd denied myself for so long. I was sure it felt so incredible because Ben and I genuinely cared about each other.

I lay awake, turning things over in my mind, and weighing up the pros and cons. There were a few things wrong.

Last night, Ben suggested he wanted more. He didn't say it, but what if he meant dating?

I couldn't honestly say I loved Ben more than I loved his brothers.

To my shame, I could've willingly gone to bed with Adam or Carl instead, and that couldn't be right. Surely, when I was in bed with the one right man for me, I shouldn't be thinking about his brothers.

If I could switch off the feelings I had for Adam and Carl, Ben seemed to suggest this might not be a one-off thing, but how could it be anything else?

If we were to date, what would that do to the family?

I couldn't be the one to come between him and his brothers when they were so close.

Us as a couple would be an odd dynamic, and it would strain relationships in the family.

Mom wouldn't be happy, and I'm not sure what his dad would think.

I just felt so confused.

Sadly, as a beautiful night turned to dawn, I slipped into feelings of despair and shame, thinking of bad words that people would call me if they saw inside my mind. I couldn't deny them. I wouldn't have gone home with just anyone, and Ben was special to me, but not enough.

I had to get out of this situation.

Much as I wanted to stay in his arms, I tried to release myself from his grip without waking him, but it didn't work.

He stirred and held me more tightly.

"Ben, I have to leave and go to my room."

His eyes shot open.

"I can turn the light off if it's too bright for you. I don't usually sleep with the light on; I just couldn't reach it to switch it off when you fell asleep on top of me."

Inside I groaned at the memory, and he mentioned it so casually.

"It's not that, Ben. I'm so sorry. I like you an awful lot, but I can't do this. We should never have done this, and I'd like just to forget it happened."

CHAPTER EIGHT
ADAM

When I entered the apartment, arriving home from college, from the doorway, I saw Carl preparing dinner in the kitchen, and I decided to go and keep him company by sitting in the living room with my textbook instead of retreating to my room to study.

"Judging by all the noise, I take it, Ben brought someone home last night? Either that or he had the volume on his porn turned up too loud."

I'd just sat down and opened a book when Carl dropped that one on me.

"I think he should be a little more considerate of Sophie in the next room. She might not like here him making a girl howl like a wolf."

Before I could reply, I heard the door open and close again. Seconds later, Ben appeared in the sitting room. He slumped at the dining table, looking like he carried the weight of the world, or had been slapped around the face by a wet fish.

"And here he is, the man who kept us awake with all the noise last night." Carl put the knife down next to his chopped veggies and rested his hands on the countertop. "I don't mind,

Ben. But you might think about keeping your female visitors a bit quieter now you've got Sophie in the next room."

"I guess things went well last night then? I didn't hear anything, Ben. But then I did get home later than you and Sophie," I said.

Ben's face was a picture. He didn't blush exactly. And he already looked a little mad before Carl went stomping in with two feet. Carl apparently hadn't picked up on Ben's foul mood and knew nothing about the woman in Ben's room last night.

I didn't need to read Ben's mind to understand; it was written across his face. Something hadn't gone well for him, and I probably shouldn't have said anything.

Carl looked at me. Did he catch on to what I was saying? Ben went home with Sophie: don't be an insensitive ass.

Ben didn't look as if he was about to say anything, but it seemed unreasonable to keep Carl in the dark. "Ben came home with Sophie, so I'm guessing it was her that you heard, Carl."

Normally when Ben arrived home, he would have gone into his room and done whatever stuff he needed to do until dinner was ready. The fact that he slumped into a chair at the table meant he had things to tell us, even if we did have to wrench it out of him with a pry bar.

"No fucking way." Carl leaned forward over the food he'd been chopping. "That was Sophie making all that noise?" He left his food preparation and walked around the kitchen island until he was standing next to Ben. Muttering quietly as he did so, "Well, I never." Then Carl pulled out a chair and sat down at the dining table. "So, what happened to you today? Why aren't you looking pleased with yourself?" Carl asked.

Ben shrugged. "Fun time was had by all. I would have liked things to have gone further. She ended us when they barely began."

Sitting in an armchair at the other end of the room, I felt far out of the loop, so I joined them at the table, pulling up a chair opposite Ben. "What do you mean to take things further? What kinky positions were you suggesting that she wasn't into?"

Ben rolled his eyes. "No, nothing like that. This morning I walked to school with her as usual, and I didn't exactly get the chance to ask if she'd like to come on a date because she cut me off before we even got into that conversation. It was a one-night stand for her. That's all." He looked miserable.

"I'm sorry, Ben. Really, I am."

She obviously meant a lot to him; just as she meant a lot to me too. I felt as gutted for him as if she'd turned me down.

"I've already texted her to say I can't meet her after class. She'll make her own way back." Ben looked down. "I... I'm gonna go out. I don't feel like having dinner with you all tonight."

Ben looked thoroughly dejected and worse and worse by the minute. He'd probably been holding it together all day, projecting his usual calm, cocky, and confident self at school.

"I hate the thought of her bringing another guy home," I confessed. I turned to Carl, who'd spent more time with her talking about art and presumably her college course. "Is she interested in any of the guys at school?"

Carl shook his head. "No, not in that way. She's made a mixed bunch of friends who she mentions from time to time. Her best buddy seems to be someone called Nathan, she mentions him a lot, but I don't know whether we need to be worried about him. She pretty much spends all of her spare time, evenings, and weekends with us."

I looked down at my fingers resting on the tabletop. "I had thought we were in with a real chance with her."

"We?" I glanced up to see Carl and Ben, both with questioning looks on their faces.

"Come on. We've talked about this. We all know we all want her. I was pleased for you both to see you go home with her last night, Ben, even though I wished it were me. If it's not me, then I'd like it to be one of you two guys."

Ben nodded. "Yeah. Funny you should say that. I thought the same thing. If she doesn't want me for anything more than a one-night stand, then I hope she'll date one of you two. I wouldn't feel bad about that."

"It's because we're used to sharing between us," Carl interrupted. "We've shared everything our whole lives; I don't know why we wouldn't share a woman too."

"You could be right. Only, I don't feel jealous if I think of one of you with her."

"Whereas if it were another dude, you'd see red." I finished the thought for him. "I'd want to rip the dudes head off and curtail his reproductive potential." I wasn't serious.

We'd talked about this before, and the conversation confirmed again that we were of one mind.

"Maybe you guys have got a chance with her, and I'd be cool with that," Ben said, and I knew he meant it. "But for whatever reason, I'm not the one for her. She's made that clear. And you know, maybe that's why. Perhaps she already prefers one of you two." He looked between us and already seemed a little more relaxed than when he first walked in.

"Well, first of all, you guys misunderstand me. I'd be happy if one of you dated her. I'd be happier if it were me. And I'd be perfectly fine with all three of us dating her," Carl explained. "It's not as if she'd be cheating if we all knew about each other. I think that would work well for us if she were into it."

"My mind has just, officially, exploded." I looked around in all directions pretending to look for blood and brains splattered on the walls. "And it was obviously empty, hence the lack of a bloody mess."

Carl chuckled.

"It's weird, Carl. I don't know anyone in real life who lives like that, but I'd be into it. Do tell me more."

"As I see it, three bros dating one girl has a lot of positive things to offer us." He sat back in his chair and looked pleased with himself before glancing at his watch. "I should take my man, Ben here, out for a burger. He's had a rough time. That will give you some alone time with her."

"Why me?" I asked.

"Because Ben usually walks her to school and I've spent plenty of time alone with her too. It's time you guys had some quality time. Just the two of you. You're a cook. Cook her dinner." Carl glanced over his shoulder. "I've made a start on the veggies, and there's a ready-cooked chicken in the fridge to go with it."

As Sophie was due home from school anytime soon, we didn't sit around analyzing the pros and cons of Carl's outrageous suggestion. Ben and Carl were up and out of the apartment within minutes.

I wasn't at all convinced that the idea of a menage with three brothers would appeal to Sophie. I certainly wasn't about to suggest it to her, but clearly, Carl had gotten out of doing dinner, and I had to step in. I took stock of the peppers and onions that were partially chopped, and I turned my attention to the contents of the fridge.

I decided to get out a tablecloth, napkins, and candles to make it just that little bit more special and romantic as it would be only the two of us. I set out wine glasses and a bottle of red.

I didn't have time to run out for fresh flowers, but the thought did cross my mind.

Once all the ingredients for dinner were laid out, and the room looked perfect, I nipped into my bathroom for a shower while I wondered what to wear.

It would appear odd if I dressed too formally for a meal that I cooked for myself in my own home, just as I had done many previous times. Awkward when Sophie didn't know we were on a date. But I wanted to make some effort. Clothes that were fresh and ironed and a clean body at least.

While I showered, I thought about what Carl had said.

We'd always lived together, assuming one day we'd move apart to live with our future wives, but living together worked well for us. It didn't make sense to think that in a few years, I'd leave the brothers I'd lived with all my life to live with someone who at this moment was a stranger to me. There wasn't anyone in my life currently who I'd consider as future wife potential, apart from Sophie.

And if it was Sophie? She seemed to get along fine with the three of us, so why shouldn't that work?

Of course, Carl wasn't suggesting the four of us living together as we do now. I didn't know about Sophie, but I knew for damn sure my brothers and I weren't ready to give up sex.

We'd never shared a girlfriend before, and while I've heard of guys involved in tag-team, group sex events, that wasn't something the three of us had ever done.

Relationships were about more than just sex, of course. But it was important. I wouldn't mind if we all did stuff separately or in the same room. There were obvious advantages as a guy only has one mouth, one tongue, and a pair of hands. I imagined what we could do if we multiplied our assets by three. I liked the thought of all of us turning her on and blowing her mind with sexy fun.

I was sitting back in the living room in clean jeans and a shirt when she arrived home. I was holding open a book I needed to read for college, but I'd read the same page over and over while finding it difficult to focus.

"Hi, Adam." Sophie slumped on the sofa next to me. "I hope Carl's on track with dinner; I'm starving. Where is he?"

She must've seen the food out and almost ready.

I stood up abruptly. "He's gone out with Ben, so I'm cooking tonight instead. It's all ready to heat up, so it'll be about ten minutes." I walked over to the kitchen area.

The chicken was already cooked. The rice needed reheating. It was just the vegetables that had to be stir-fried, and the salad brought out from the fridge.

As I placed the salad bowl on the table, she seemed to notice for the first time the table linen.

She stood up, came over, and sat in her usual seat. "This is very nice. What's the occasion?" She asked.

"I hope you don't mind, the occasion is that it's only you and me. Our first dinner alone. I thought it would be nice to make an effort to make it special."

"Ah." She smiled warmly. "It's lovely. Your cooking is always so delicious; we should always have a fancy tablecloth so that it feels like we're in a restaurant."

"Well, without the silver service. And I'd feel under pressure to deliver something amazing every time. You know, arranging it on the plate instead of plonking it on in dollops."

"I don't mind dollops." She ran her fingers through her hair, holding onto a strand and wrapping it around her finger. "I don't need everything done for me."

"I know. You're far more independent than your mother knows." I poured a little sesame oil into the wok.

She cocked her head to one side and smiled. In stark contrast to Ben earlier, Sophie seemed perfectly cheerful. She was positively beaming.

"Why you so happy?" I asked.

"What's not to be happy about? I live with three lovely guys who look after me in every way."

"Hey, when you cook, it's delicious too." I scraped every last piece of colorful vegetable from the chopping board into the pan.

"Well, it easy to make an effort when I've only got to cook once every four days. It seems the perfect living arrangement. I can't believe we've only lived together for a few weeks, and I can't imagine a future in which I don't live with you three."

"I feel the same." I was itching to ask her about what happened between her and Ben. After all, the last time I saw her, she was holding his hand and about to leave with him, but having seen Ben's face earlier, I couldn't ask her.

So far, we hadn't developed the sort of relationship in which we'd share that kind of conversation, and. I couldn't help thinking Carl should be with her right now, rather than me.

I opened the bottle of wine to calm my nerves and help break the ice between us.

Her eyes widened. "You boys never drink."

"And you exaggerate. It's not never."

"Well, rarely, then."

I walked around to pour her a glass of wine too.

"I'm just going to wash my hands if dinner won't be long."

CHAPTER NINE
SOPHIE

As I rinsed the soap from my hands, I looked down at my clothes and noticed the fine coating of charcoal dust, evidence of the artistic technique I'd been practicing that day. It must have been five minutes earlier when Adam announced we had ten minutes until dinner, so I figured I had five minutes to transform myself. If I put my hair up so that it didn't get wet, I could take two minutes in the shower, two minutes for drying, and one minute to get dressed.

I freshened up in great haste and felt better for knowing dinner would be on the table any second. I slipped into the first dress I laid my hands on, reasoning a dress would be faster than a separate top and bottom. And Adam had made an effort, and it would be nice if I dressed up for the occasion too.

I was both relieved and disappointed that Ben wasn't home. Relieved, I wouldn't have to face him and disappointed that I wouldn't see him. After what happened the night before and the way he looked so deflated after our conversation when I said we should forget it, I was eager to get back to a status of normality in our relationship.

"You've changed. You look nice." Judging by the way Adam looked at me when I re-entered the dining area, he approved of my dress choice. I liked the way his eyes roved over my appearance. He began dishing up the hot food. "I'm going for the plonked on the plate approach again."

"It's how it tastes that counts." I sat down once again in my usual seat.

Having a candlelit dinner alone with Adam wasn't normal. I acted casual, but I couldn't help feeling like we were on a date. It felt sweet, fun, and romantic, and it churned up all the emotions that I felt toward each one of these brothers. I liked them all more than I should and wouldn't want to spoil what we had or choose between them.

While we ate, Adam asked about my day at art school.

"I'm experimenting with different materials and techniques. Today was charcoal."

"What was that like?" He nodded and seemed interested in what I had to say.

"Done right, it can give a terrific effect. It projects an atmosphere. I worked on pictures of spooky buildings. It's great for that atmospheric effect, but charcoal can be a difficult medium to use because it's so easy to smudge and ruin the picture, and charcoal is just so damned messy."

"Do you think you'll use it often? Will it become a weapon in your arsenal?"

"I don't think so. I'm going to give it more of a chance. It's good to have an understanding of different tools, but I don't see me doing much with charcoal."

I paused to sip my wine between eating and talking. I wasn't an experienced drinker. I could taste the fruity highlights, but the bitterness overpowered all else, and it was an effort to drink the red wine that Adam had poured for me. To keep him company, I drank some wine and far more of the water which I'd gotten for myself.

"What about you, what have you been doing today?" I asked politely because I knew Adam had been at college, and everything about his business management course sounded dull.

"Ah, well, we're looking at motivation theory at the moment."

I must have looked blank. "What's that?"

"What motivates us to do we do the things we do. It's fascinating," he said with a surprising amount of enthusiasm.

"That does sound interesting."

"Yes, it is. Understanding and using the theory can help predict customer actions and motivate staff."

I screwed up my face like I was sucking a lemon. "And the application doesn't sound as interesting as the subject."

Fortunately, Adam wasn't offended. He'd gotten used to my blunt-talking and laughed along with me.

"I hoped you were going to explain why I do the things I do. It would be great to be able to understand people like that."

"Agreed. I'm too new to the subject to come back with an answer. Or better yet, why don't you just tell me what motivates you, Sophie."

I looked at the ceiling for an answer. "What motivates me? It depends on the situation. I was motivated to study art because I enjoy it, and I'm good at it. Is that an answer?"

Adam rested his arm on the table and cocked his head to one side. "I guess I'm more interested in what your motives are around Ben, and Carl, and me."

With each passing day, it was harder to suppress the knowledge that I was very attracted to each and every one of these guys. Now I'd had a taste of Ben, literally, I was so curious to find out if that was a one-off or whether sexy times with each brother would be just as good.

"Oh." I swallowed. I knew my face went bright red; I felt it heat up. "I didn't expect you to ask me about Ben. I thought he might have told you." I thought Ben would be relieved when I told him we should just carry on as normal as if nothing had happened, but he looked really disappointed.

Adam didn't respond, didn't move. Before the silence became uncomfortable, I felt compelled to say more. "Last night, I was motivated by lust, and then motivated by common sense when I left his room instead of staying there. Is that what you wanted to know? Do they have a theory about sleeping with the wrong person?"

"Ben didn't feel the same way. I mean, about you being the wrong person." There was a small, almost imperceptible change to Adam's expression. He then sat up a little straighter. "If I could tell you what motivates people in one simple short answer, I'd be a very rich man. I think the purpose of the course is to make it clear that motives and aims are not always obvious or logical. So people don't always do what you might expect them to."

I felt relieved we didn't linger on my love life, and Adam moved the conversation on to more comfortable ground. "Oh.

I can think of many examples of that. Or maybe I'm just bad at guessing what people will do because they always surprise me."

"Like I'm going to surprise you now, by suggesting cocktails. I haven't got dessert, but I can rustle up surprising sweet drinks for after dinner."

I hadn't finished the first glass of wine. I deliberately didn't look at it.

I was tempted to say I'd try anything once, but I didn't think it was the right time for that comment, given what we'd just said about Ben. "I'm happy to give your cocktail a try. Although I should say, I don't have much experience of cocktails." I didn't have any.

"Fear not. No prior experience necessary. You go and take a comfortable seat on the sofa in front of the TV and choose something for us to watch." Adam picked up the empty plates. "I'll be over in a minute with your alcoholic after-dinner beverage."

I was already buzzing from the evening of delicious food and pleasant company. I hadn't finished a glass of wine, so I'd say the alcohol wasn't to blame.

I'd also been on a terrific high all day after the night before. I didn't exactly regret sleeping with Ben because it had been an amazing experience, which gave me a lasting high. I wanted to do the same thing again and soon. I didn't let myself dwell on the fact that I couldn't be with one of my stepbrothers. Ben and I couldn't be an item. We wouldn't do that again.

When it came to motivation, I guessed I was an optimist who focused on the slither of silver lining that I could see, rather than the vast gray-black storm cloud.

I'd heard it said that sex, exercise, and laughter were three things that can elevate a person's mood, so much so that it might lift them out of depression. Certainly, my first time with Ben had a great impact on my subsequent mood. It had been good enough to put a smile on my face for the day. I loved it and wanted more.

After leaving the table, I sat on the sofa and turned on the TV. I was still channel surfing when Adam came to my side. He handed me a drink and sat down beside me.

Raising the glass to my nose, I sniffed at the rim before carefully taking a sip. It didn't hit me like other alcoholic drinks, and I could've believed it was soda. I took a big gulp. It was extremely sweet and tasted of almonds.

"Easy there, don't let it fool you. There is plenty of alcohol between those bubbles."

I raised my glass. "Cheers then," and took another sip, a smaller one this time.

"Here's to charcoal and motivation." Adam raised his glass and clinked it against mine. I didn't expect it and almost spilled some. Fortunately, I had a good grip on the glass but decided to pace myself by placing it on the table. He did the same with his drink.

"So what are we watching?" he asked.

"You haven't got to study motivation tonight?"

"Perhaps later. I can afford some unwind time."

"We'll unwind together." I honestly couldn't blame it on the alcoholic buzz, so instead, I'd blame it on the high from the night before because I felt playfully like mucking about as I would from time to time with my younger sisters. For some reason, I swung a leg across him. Without planning anything, I found myself sitting on his lap, facing him.

"That's it. I've got you." Giggling, I had him pinned to the sofa. "Explain your motivation behind giving me that drink."

"Um." Naturally, I'd taken him completely by surprise. "Did you say you were ticklish?" Threateningly, he placed his hands on my waist. "Because if so, you'll want to surrender."

I wiggled on top of him. "Even though I'm on higher ground? I will not surrender. You're my prisoner."

Taking the lead, my physically driven instincts overcoming rational logic, I kissed him. Kissing Adam was not something I deliberately set out to do. And when it happened, I was as shocked by it as him. I could only blame my wanton, lust filled body, which wanted to experience more touches like those of the night before.

I had to blame something.

My motivation may have been driven by curiosity or just straightforward desire. I felt a strong attraction toward him and, well, kissing just happened. I didn't need to analyze my actions. Just do them.

Nevertheless, I didn't stop, and his mouth welcomed mine. His head went right back, and I plundered his mouth with my kisses. We were doing this on my initiative and not his, and I enjoyed the feeling of being dominant over him.

He slipped his hands away from my waist, running them up and down my back while I weaved my fingers through his hair. Slowly his hands came to rest on the cheeks of my ass.

When I became aware of his erection, I liked it even more. I liked turning him on, and knowing I did that to him. And I liked the way his cock felt against my crotch as I rocked against him. I pressed my pussy down harder against his groin.

Heat rushed through me when Adam's hands progressed from behind me, slowly moving forward to sit on my exposed thighs. Only then did I realized how much my dress had ridden up because of my position. It barely concealed anything. I'd never have the nerve to dress in a way that was revealing deliberately.

With my legs wide apart as I straddled him, I was both on top and in control but also vulnerable and exposed. I wouldn't have wanted anything any different.

I moaned, which must have revealed my thoughts as my hips moved slightly, rubbing my crotch against his, making clear my arousal. I knew I could stop this at any time. I knew I should. I knew stopping wasn't going to happen.

I'd wanted this so much. I'd initiated it. And now we were so close, I was hardly going to get up and walk away.

I noticed him looking down at my thighs too, and I think I detected a wicked glint in his eyes. "Is this all right?" His fingers slipped under the hem of my dress and between my legs.

"Yes," I painted. My ragged breath betrayed my desires.

My panties were probably as wet as they were when Ben had removed them.

As this was my second journey into such intimacy, I felt a little less paranoid about my moisture than I did the day before.

Adam must have liked finding me so wet as he moaned with pleasure when his fingers made contact with the wet cotton of my panties. I felt him push the gusset to one side. And I moaned with excitement when his strong fingers stroked up and down my pussy, over my sensitive clit, and in between my folds.

"Oh," I sighed.

I wished my dress would evaporate with my underwear too.

I wanted to sit on his lap now like this, but naked, exposed, and wanton so that he would proceed to ravish me on the sofa.

Maybe he could read my mind as his fingers invaded my entrance, probing into the passage, and making me moan.

CHAPTER TEN
ADAM

When I began to cook dinner, I had no idea I'd be having Sophie for dessert.

She was rightfully due for a little romance, and I hoped we'd get to know each other better, but I didn't expect things to move so fast.

It took our first time alone to discover the chemistry between us. We couldn't have stayed apart if we wanted to.

When I moved my hands in between her thighs and found my way inside her panties, I wasn't trying to conquer just another woman. I felt it was entirely a privilege to be allowed to touch her like that more than anything I wanted to make it good for her.

Feeling how wet and turned on she'd become took me by surprise. And it sure felt reassuring to know that she was as excited as me.

In fact, her enthusiastic arousal was probably what got me so worked up.

"You're so beautiful like this, Sophie." She had me trapped where I sat. And I had no intention of wrestling her off even though it did restrict what we could do. Who was complaining? I had some pretty good options.

She threw her head back with laughter, and I took the opportunity to suck and nibble on her exposed throat, which made her squirm on top of me, moisture flowing out over my fingers.

I pushed my fingers in to satisfy her hot need.

This could just be the hottest thing that ever happened to me, and I couldn't believe I'd gotten so lucky.

"Would you like to get more comfortable?" I asked.

"Why? Are you uncomfortable?"

"Well, I could certainly do with lying down."

She laughed.

"I'm thinking, if I were to lie down here, you could sit across my face. And lose the panties first."

"Oh." I saw a look of surprise and delight on her face. She wiggled back toward my knees and then stood up.

I reached up under her dress and pulled down her panties. When she stepped out of them, and I picked them up and put them in my pocket.

Without getting up, I swiveled around on the sofa. I also flicked the buttons on my fly because, frankly, my dick ached; it was painful trapped in there.

She stood beside me.

As I realized she was watching, I decided to make a little show of it. I laid back on the sofa, I raised my ass in the air and gave a little wriggle as I pushed my jeans and underwear down just a little bit, freeing up my erection.

She licked her lips.

And I licked mine.

"You like looking at this?" I held my cock between my thumb and fingers and ran my fingers up and down the shaft from the route to the tip. I stroked around the glands and back down, slowly teasing myself and teasing her with the visuals.

She licked her lips again and nodded.

She was lost for words.

I liked seeing her this way.

Pointing a finger at my lips, I said, "Come and get on," in what I hoped was an irresistible, sexy deep voice.

She looked unsure. She was free, of course, to say no.

Perhaps all she needed was clarification about what I had in mind. I knew exactly what I wanted.

Waving toward my shoulder, I explained, "Put your knees either side of me."

"Okay, I'll give it a go." She seemed eager and did what I suggested straightaway.

She tasted heavenly, like the best dessert flavor ever. Her wet and swollen pussy opened up and welcomed me.

I ran my tongue up and down her slit, probing between the soft, puffy skin and lapping up some of the excess moisture.

Giving her pleasure tasted so good.

My finger slipped underneath her and found the warm moist entrance. I slipped in a finger while my tongue licked over and around her tempting bud.

Sensing the arousal rising in her the from way she rocked and her breathing turned me on more and more, too.

While she rubbed herself against my chin, I placed a hand on my needy cock. Precum pooled on my stomach. I swiped my fingers through it and used it as lube. I rubbed my fingers back and forth, providing the much-needed friction that it ached for.

There was no way to telling her right then, in that position, how much she turned me on.

Together we simply had chemistry. I wanted to give her everything and to make her feel special. I wanted her to come and to know how close I was, too.

The rub and thrust against my face suddenly changed pace, and my mouth filled with her gushing juices. They tasted heavenly as evidence of her climax.

I could hold back no longer. I held my hand still, and my cock pulsed between my fingers.

It took several seconds, maybe a minute or two before we both returned from that heightened state of ecstasy to become conscious of our surroundings.

She rose and stood beside the sofa, looking a little shaky on her feet. As she stood up, her dress fell back over her legs, covering her decently.

As I was still dressed, I mopped up using the shirt I was wearing. I rubbed my hands on my pants and wiped my mouth with my sleeve. I must've looked a mess. Standing up, I tucked myself away,

and pulled up my pants, while feeling fan-fucking-tastic and very much in need of a shower.

"That was amazing, Sophie. And that's the understatement of the year. Thank you." I took her hand in mine, stepped toward her, and planted a kiss on her mouth.

Her lips opened slightly to welcome mine. Slowly our tongues got involved too. They met and entered each other's mouths to taste and explore. It seemed more intense and intimate than the kiss we'd shared earlier.

I wrapped my hands around her and held her in my arms. And inside, my heart felt full of something. Love, I guessed. It couldn't have just been lust because my primal urges had been sated for now. This was a different urge. Just wanting to hold her and be with her. It went well with my desire to look after her and care for her, into the future.

We kissed for what seemed like many minutes until we withdrew apart for air.

"I didn't expect that for afters." She smiled playfully. She really was an incredible woman.

"That particular dessert is on the menu every day of the week for you. You only have to ask."

"Well, I might just do that."

I wondered what next. I wasn't sure what to say about our relationship. Just when I hoped she'd take the lead, we heard the door the front door click and voices at the threshold. They stopped talking almost immediately as if they'd been talking outside but stopped so that we wouldn't hear their conversation on entering the apartment.

Shortly, Carl appeared in the doorway. "Hi," he said. "Good evening here?" And with barely a glance in our direction, he walked to the kitchen and helped himself to a drink of water.

"All is just great," said Sophie. "I'm going to bed." She looked at me and then walked off to her room, leaving me completely unsure about where I stood.

Should I follow her? Should I go to my room?
Should I send her a text from my room?

Ben didn't make an appearance; he'd presumably gone straight to his room, and it seemed as if he were avoiding Sophie.

Before I made a decision, Carl was back on my side of the kitchen island and walking toward me with his eyes running up and down my clothes.

I suddenly became very self-conscious about my appearance.

"For a minute there, I thought you'd spilled food down your shirt. I'm not wanting to think about it being something else." He stopped coming toward me. "Reassure me, bro. Because some things you can't unsee."

"Fine," I said. "We mucked about on the sofa, fighting over the TV remote. I spilled the dessert."

Carl had already turned away. "Good. I'm glad things went well for you."

CHAPTER ELEVEN
SOPHIE

The bike screeched to a sudden halt. The rider put a foot down on the tarmac. "Hey, Sophie. You're here early."

"As if I don't know it." I rested my sketch pad and pencil on my knees. "And what's your excuse?"

Nathan got off his bike and pushed it over toward the bench where I was sitting.

"I just seem to be ahead of myself this morning, so I thought I'd get here early. It might give me the chance to dish out some fliers. And you, what are you doing here?"

"Same. Just ahead of myself." I didn't want to tell Nathan that I hurried out of the house without speaking to anyone this morning. I left a note for Ben, who normally walked to school with me, telling him I'd left.

After my dinner date with Adam, I felt more confused than ever. I didn't think I could stand to walk and chat with Ben.

"What fliers are you handing out?"

Nathan sat down on the bench next to me and rummaged in his messenger bag. "These," he said, pulling out a scrap of paper. "It's not what it looks like. I know it looks like me handing out my phone number to hot guys I'd like to see naked." Nathan grinned.

I looked at the flier seeking life models and laughed. "Oh, I see. It looks a lot like a ploy to find guys and get them naked."

"Such is the life of an artist. It's a tough job, but someone has to do it." Nathan fanned his face with his hand. "And speaking of hot guys, where's that stepbrother of yours? He's normally beside you every morning when you arrive. He watches over you like a furious bodyguard. Has he already gone?"

I blushed at the connection.

"Don't worry. Soph, I didn't say I wanted to see him naked."

I guessed I was no good at keeping secrets because Nathan looked at my face and did a clear double take.

"Sophie, is there something you want to tell me? And does it involve your naked brother?"

"Stepbrother, if you don't mind," I insisted. The distinction was very important here and now. "It's embarrassing."

"Darling, there's nothing you can say that will be more embarrassing than some of the stuff I've done. We can compete for who's done the most embarrassing shit if you like. But believe me, you won't shock me. Okay," Nathan drew the last word out extremely slowly. "Tell me about your naked stepbrother."

I cringed as I said, "Stepbrothers, Nathan. My naked stepbrothers. Plural."

"Oh, my god, Soph!" he screeched.

"Nathan, I slept with Ben." If we were going to have this competition, I would pull out my top-scoring card straight away. Sure enough, he was stumped. His eyeballs looked ready to jump out of his face, and for once, Nathan's mouth fell open; he was lost for words. "Do I win? We didn't agree on a prize, did we?"

"Okay, you've got me there. I was not expecting that," Nathan replied. "I'm gonna have to dig deep to find something embarrassing to top that one but don't worry, I will."

I shook my head. "Oh, it doesn't end there, Nathan. There's more."

Nathan vibrated with excitement. "You didn't! Tell me, you did? Are we talking all three together? Because my brain can't cope with a story that hot this early."

Despite my embarrassment, I couldn't help laughing. Nathan was so excited and always funny. It was what I liked about him.

"Nathan, I think I've messed up."

He pushed his flier back into the bag without taking his eyes off my face. "I expect it's easy for things to go very wrong if you start having threesomes with your brothers. Oh, wait, there are three of them. Scratch that, foursomes with your brothers."

"Stepbrothers. And there were no threesomes or foursomes, but damn, Nathan. I didn't need that thought in my mind."

I proceeded to recite how I'd slept with Ben the night before last and then laughed it off as if it were no big deal. Only after I told him, it seemed pretty plain from the look on Ben's face that it was a big deal to him.

"I didn't know what to do or say because it was a big deal for me too, but it's not as if we can start dating."

"I don't see why not." Nathan appeared to be agog for more of this story. "But you haven't told me about naked stepbrothers, plural, yet."

"Last night, I had a romantic dinner, just Adam and me, and one thing led to another."

Nathan's eye grew to the size of saucers, almost as big as his wide open mouth. "You slept with another brother. That's two, two nights in a row."

"We didn't exactly sleep, Nate. In fact, I went off to my bed, and he went to his. He did send some very sweet texts to me in the night." I ran my hand through my hair and let out a big sigh. "I didn't get to say the wrong thing to Adam last night because he left me in no doubt that he wants more."

"More sex?"

"No, well, maybe." I giggled. "I mean, he wants a relationship. It was kind of clear when we were together, and then he spelled it out in the messages."

"Can I see them?"

I hadn't expected that. "No. They're private."

"Oh." Nathan sat back and tilted his head to give me one of the side-eye looks.

"Not private like that. I mean, they were just intended for me. They weren't crude; they were sweet. And he says he wants a relationship of some sort with me."

Nathan tapped his fingers on the side of his messenger bag. "So, your problem is he doesn't know you slept with his brother just the night before?"

"No. He knows about that. It doesn't seem to bother him. He knows Ben wants a relationship with me too, but we didn't get to talk about that."

"I see. Your family life is wilder than a story on the Jerry Springer show. So what do you want to do about it?"

"I have no idea. I like them both. In fact, I like all three triplets equally. If I had to choose, I think it would be impossible, and it would just ruin things as we all get along so well now."

"Do you want my opinion?" asked Nathan.

Did I? I didn't think so, but it looked like he was going to give it to me anyway, so I politely nodded. "Yes. What do you think?"

"You know us gay boys have an undeserved reputation for being sluts. And I, for one, certainly like to play up to the stereotype of gay boy who's easy." He placed both of his hands on his chest. "But, Soph, there's sleeping around, and then there's taking it beyond all limits of decency known to mankind. I think having a relationship with your stepbrother is over the line. But with two or three of them, that is over the top."

"I wasn't thinking of dating all three of them," I protested.

"Weren't you? Because that's how it sounded to me. You can't choose. You like them equally. And, honey, if the other two look like Ben, I'd be offering myself up to all three of them if I got the chance."

"Hey, now. Wait a minute. How come you can have a fantasy foursome with my boys and I can't? That sounds a bit sexist. What's the opposite of homophobic that means fear of straight group stuff?"

Nathan laughed with his hand on his stomach as if I'd said something terribly funny.

"What is it, Nate?"

"I don't care how many boys you have at one time, Soph. All power to you if you can do that. The problem is they're your stepbrothers. That doesn't bother me either, but what'll your collective parents think?"

I shrugged.

"If your parents are anything like mine, then they'll blame each other. And they'll fight. A lot. You'll be blamed by the boys' dad for seducing them. Your mom will blame the boys for corrupting you, and she'll blame their dad for the boys' terrible morals. It'll turn out to be a big family bust-up."

I completely agreed with Nathan's assessment of the situation. "I thought that too. And that's if I only dated one of them. None of them has said they'd be happy if I dated two or three of them at the same time. We just haven't had that conversation. I've never heard of that happening."

"Sophie, I love you to pieces, but sometimes you are all small-town, sheltered-life, girlfriend. I know a few people who've been down some sort of open relationship or menage path. Those things are more common than you'd realize. People probably just don't always announce it, so you wouldn't know."

I shook my head. Not disagreeing, but trying to dislodge the mental block I had over what Nathan was saying. "So, in these group relationships, don't people get jealous?"

"Apparently not, I'm no expert. I haven't done it myself."

"I can't see how it would work."

"Well, I guess everyone involves discussed what they want, and they set ground rules. Much like a two-person relationship." Nathan glanced at his watch. "This has certainly been fun, but we need to get to class, and I've got to get my bike locked up."

We stood up.

"Thanks for your wisdom, Nathan."

CHAPTER TWELVE
CARL

We never told Dad about Ben's gay-bar go-go dancing days. Dad wouldn't approve. He thought Adam's DJ job was a waste of time and talent, but Adam still managed to get top scores for all his papers so Dad couldn't grumble too much.

Then there was me — the youngest. I'd always been up for anything in the art world.

I went out on wedding photography shoots a few times as a volunteer assistant. That was interesting, but not enough for me to want to do it on a regular basis. Weddings could be pretty boring.

I'd entered every local photography exhibition or competition for which I was eligible, and that had turned out to be quite a few. So I'd sold some photos and won about twenty dollars in prize money.

Naturally, in my first year of college, I put my name down when they required life models for the art courses. A surprisingly large number of people were willing to take their clothes off in front of complete strangers for relatively little money, so I hadn't been called upon that often. I sit for a class a few times each semester.

My brothers and I threw ourselves into extracurricular activities. We could afford to try out many things, whether they paid well or not. We were fortunate that we didn't depend on the money from our part-time jobs.

We didn't need the money, but life was about experiences, and we wanted to pack them in.

That was how come Adam had a DJ slot at a nightclub. He enjoyed it, but never wanted to make a career of it. He didn't need the cash, so he didn't take on the later, more lucrative slots.

Ben often went along with Adam. He liked to dance. A few times, he was paid to dance at the club where Adam worked when they had special themed parties. After that, he went on to get a part-time job as a go-go dancer in a gay bar. That was a lot of fun. Even I went there a few times. I wasn't gay, Ben and Adam weren't either, but the guys in that bar loved the three of us, and we had some good nights out.

I had a feeling it would be Sophie's class that I'd be sitting for today.

She'd mentioned a number of times that she'd be sketching naked people. We'd had the conversation on numerous evenings. I think Sophie was a little nervous or excited, and it was hard to say.

In all honesty, I knew I should have mentioned something about me doing that kind of work, even if I didn't realize it was going to be for her class, but I didn't mention it. Ben and Adam both looked at me, expecting me to say something, but they didn't say anything either.

I wasn't nervous about taking my clothes off.

I'd done it before, and getting naked in front of strangers was fun for about a minute or less, while I watched the artist's faces and reactions. However, it was interesting to see their finished work at the end of the sessions.

The rest of the time was quite dull and sometimes even physically exhausting and stressful.

Once the session was underway, holding poses, staying completely still, even for just a minute or two, often seemed like forever. The most comfortable position started to feel uncomfortable after five minutes, and unfortunately, those were the ones I'd have to hold for twenty minutes at a time, have a brief break, and then return.

It all begged the question of why I kept doing it. I didn't voice my complaints aloud precisely because of this matter. Most of the influx of nude models would drop out after only one sitting when they realized they couldn't face the boredom and discomfort. My ego wouldn't let me quit. Instead, I made sure I did the fewest number of sitting possible each semester. Usually, two.

The students were already at their drawing boards when I entered the room. I'd already removed my clothes and only wore a robe.

I wasn't completely sure this was Sophie's class, but I made eye contact with her immediately and saw the surprise on her face.

Why hadn't I expected that?

And she obviously hadn't expected to see me.

The art teacher asked me to stand comfortably in front of them.

When I shed my robe, I didn't look at Sophie, but thoughts went through my head about her. In the past two days, she'd slept with one of my brothers; precise details remained unconfirmed. Last night, evidence suggested something happened with the other brother. That food didn't end up on Adam's shirt by itself.

Now, there I was, in front of her.

I never had an erection while posing for life drawing classes. There was nothing sexy about it at all. However, standing naked in front of Sophie was a different matter. That was erotic, and enough to get every part of me standing up at attention.

Unwanted thoughts rushed through my head about her enjoying a romantic candlelit dinner with one of my brothers and the noisy sex I'd overheard. It had given me plenty of fantasy fodder the last couple of nights.

In fact, since she moved in, I had been jerking off on a daily basis with impure thoughts about Sophie.

And now I was standing naked in front of her.

It took all my concentration to keep the blood out of my cock. And keep all sexy thoughts out of my mind. I had to focus, instead, on our president's fiscal policies as a necessary distraction.

I changed positions when the teacher requested. The artists looked at me and sketched. Eventually, I stopped thinking about Sophie and drifted off into that day-dreamy place that I usually found. The announcement of break time came as a sudden but welcome interruption.

Barely had I wrapped my robe around me than a young dude was standing in front of me with a scrap of paper in his hand. He was skinny and wore trendy clothes that appeared to be two sizes too small. I didn't know how he got in them, and I felt like a colossal lumbering oaf in front of him.

He raised the paper toward me, but before he could speak, Sophie strode across the room and abruptly pushed the dude's hand away.

"What are you doing here? And why didn't you tell me you are going to be here?" She addressed me and completely ignored the other guy.

My brain had dulled, overpowered by monotony, because I didn't respond quickly.

"Introductions, Sophie. You've never formally introduced your brother," said the artistic dude.

I wondered how this guy knew we were related, to some extent.

"Stepbrother, Nathan," Sophie snapped. "You've never met this one." She continued looking at me, anger in her eyes, while she spoke to him. "This is Carl. Carl, this is Nathan."

"I'm pleased to meet you. I think it's safe to say I'm, perhaps, Sophie's best friend at school." The young guy, who was quite possibly a year younger than Sophie, waved his hand between the two of us. "You didn't know each other was going to be here?" He seemed oblivious to Sophie's mood, but he focused on me and didn't even glance at her.

"No," she replied.

I shook my head.

Finally, my brain caught up, and it was time to defend myself. "This is my third year of modeling at this college. I didn't realize you were going to be in this class."

The small guy, Nathan, raised his hand again. "I need a life model. The sessions will be in this building, and I can afford to pay the going rate if you are interested."

I reached out and took the paper with his details. "Thanks."

"If you would consider doing just one session, that would be great."

"Nathan! He's one of my stepbrothers," Sophie protested.

And Nathan looked as confused by this statement as I felt.

"I'm only offering him work for an hour or two, Sophie. I don't know why you're getting your panties in a twist."

"Nor me. Sophie, I understand, you're surprised to see me, but we've only lived together for a few weeks, and I don't think you know everything about us."

As soon as I'd said it, I hated that I'd said about us, instead of about me. Ignorant people, who didn't know us, would often lump us together as if three triplets equaled one whole person. We triplets fiercely fought to be recognized as individuals when we looked so alike. We were individual men with our own minds and motives.

Yet, often in our day to day lives, we thought of ourselves as a cohesive group rather than as individuals. I supposed it was a bit like how some married couples who lived together for years talk about themselves as a couple rather than an individual. But we weren't a couple. We were more like a fraternity or a sports team — a group of players who had similar goals and spent a lot of time together.

Sophie and I had spent time together. But she didn't know me as well as she may have thought, and she didn't know my brothers either. I was still hurting because of how she rejected Ben. Her rejection of one of us felt like a rejection of all of us.

It was crazy, but emotions are always crazy, not logical.

"Nathan, do you mind if I have a private word with Carl?"

All the students had stepped outside for the break by this time, to go to the bathroom, the vending machines, or to get air. We three were the only people still in the room.

I always preferred to stay in the classroom for the break. It was for a relatively short time, and walking around college dressed in nothing more than a robe didn't appeal.

"Sure," he said, both his hands flew up in the air at this point, and he backed out of the door, leaving Sophie and me alone in the classroom.

When the door shut behind him, I began my half-hearted apology. "It was just another modeling session to me, but I should have thought about the fact that you might be here." I didn't have anything to be sorry about, except that I'd upset her. There was nothing wrong with what I was doing.

"You should've. Didn't you think about how shocked and embarrassed I might be to see you like this?"

No. I knew that wasn't the correct answer.

"I'm sorry, Sophie. I'll be honest, I never thought about that. You were going to be drawing somebody, and it just happens to be me. What difference does that make?"

Her cheeks flushed red. "Isn't it obvious?" She looked around; I followed her gaze about the classroom, confirming we were alone. "I expected it to be someone old and someone I didn't know. Not somebody young and handsome."

Her hands went to her mouth as if to stop herself speaking. She hung her head and looked at the floor. "I don't know. I can't do this right now. All three of you are so attractive, and I like all of you."

It was a weird situation, and a full hug seemed inappropriate under the circumstances. I placed a hand on her shoulder.

"Look, Sophie, my brothers and I, we all find you attractive. We'd all like to date you. You can choose any one of us or, frankly, we wouldn't mind sharing you either."

At that comment, she looked up. Surprised, shocked, or disbelieving, I wasn't sure what crossed through her mind.

"We're used to sharing," I said, in case she didn't fully understand my meaning.

I would have liked to talk more, but the door opened, and a few students walked in. She walked away to stand behind her easel, where she began to fiddle with pencils. I turned my attention away from her to watch the other students. They were so deeply engaged in their conversations it was as if they didn't see me. That was fine by me.

As anyone who'd done life modeling knew, the final minutes stretch out, lasting hours. I stood and sat in many positions, becoming increasingly uncomfortable and numb.

I focused elsewhere. In my head, I certainly had stuff to think about.

CHAPTER THIRTEEN
SOPHIE

After approaching Carl during the break, I couldn't face a second conversation. I kept an eye on the clock, and when class ended, I was packed up and out of the door faster than anyone. I charged out of the classroom, desperate to get away.

Somehow, over the course of the lesson, I made a life-changing decision, one that required action.

With one destination in mind, I dashed along the corridor and down the stairs.

"Sophie, wait up." I could hear Nathan tearing after me, and as I walked downstairs, he reached my side. He didn't say anything else. We were going at such a pace neither of us had the breath for conversation. We went down the stairs and outside. I walked toward the administration offices in the next building, and Nathan stayed alongside me.

When I reached the door of the director of residential life, my can-do attitude suffered a little. The door was shut and displayed a definitive closed sign. On closer inspection, the timetable on the door revealed they opened in an hour, just when my next class was due to start.

Since first seeing Carl in my art class until that moment, I had been on high alert with my body tensed for fight or flight. I turned to face Nathan and felt my shoulders slump.

"So, that's your plan, is it? You're going to look for somewhere else to live?"

Nodding, I replied, "It's the only solution. I don't know how I'll face the three of them again, and it seems there's too much temptation in the house."

"Temptation for them? Or temptation for you?"

I smiled, shrugged again, and shook my head. I had no answer. At least, not one I wanted to share. "Come on."

As we turned to leave, Nathan suddenly grabbed my arm. "But look, there's a notice board." He pointed at the wall opposite the door we'd been staring at.

The largest notice stated that all the college-owned, on-site student accommodation was currently full. I was disappointed, but not completely surprised by this. However, there were also ads for apartments and roommates further afield.

I pulled out my phone and began to take photographs of the ads. Many were probably unsuitable, such as the one that specifically mentioned it was a house full of men. No, I definitely didn't want that. I'd probably do better staying where I was than moving in with a bunch of dudes I didn't know.

At least I currently lived with guys who make me feel safe. Then I remembered that was a big part of the problem. The guys I lived with were supposedly family. I reheard Carl's voice in my head. What did he mean when he said they'd be happy to share me? What exactly did that mean?

Speaking of sharing, it was my turn to cook that night.

"I've got a plan. I'm going to call these numbers." I held my phone aloft and gave it a shake. "I'll skip classes this afternoon and hang around for when the accommodation office opens to see if they've got anything else."

If there was a chance of finding somewhere, I needed to act fast and check it out. Ideally, I'd be home and have dinner cooked before the rest of them arrived back so that we didn't end up hanging out together.

Sitting in and sharing our evening meals had been pleasant, and now the thought of doing it again was terrifying.

"Let's go get a drink," he said. "And you can tell me about your plans."

The hour passed quickly, talking to Nathan, plotting with him, and calling the telephone numbers I'd photographed on the wall.

I didn't make it to the housing office that day because I got lucky with two of the numbers I called. I found myself with appointments to look at rooms. The first was that afternoon, which would mean missing class, and the second in the evening.

The house in turned out to be a little further from school than where I currently lived. I could conceivably continue to walk to school if I wanted to get the exercise, but I'd probably have to allow more than thirty minutes. Or I could take up the offer my mom and stepdad made to buy me a car.

It had seemed extravagant. My stepbrothers each had cars but rarely drove them as we lived so central. I think they might have routinely driven to school before I moved in. None of them mentioned it after I went off on a monologue stating that it would be appalling lazy and bad for the environment given that we lived so close to our college campuses as well as just about everywhere we might want to go.

As far as I knew, Carl and Adam did drive to their classes, but we didn't talk about it; we had no reason to have that discussion. The boys all did serious sounding business courses, and their classes were at a different college than mine. We didn't run into each other in the day, usually. Ben generally walked with me most of the time, but went out of his way to do so.

Sometimes, however, I had a lot of art materials to cart around, making a car a practical necessity. That occurred more often than I cared to admit.

When I knocked on the door, it was opened immediately as if the woman had been waiting just on the other side.

"Hi, I'm Elisha, you must be Sophie?" She opened the door wide and welcomed me in. She had a warm smiling face, and her eyes sparkled with cheerfulness.

"Yes, that's right." I stepped into a long narrow hallway. This only made it seem even stranger that she was behind the door by chance when I knocked. "I've come to see the room. Just in case lots of people called Sophie are coming to your house today."

She grinned. "Yeah, I knew it was you. You're the only Sophie I'm expecting." She set off along the corridor and up the stair, saying as she went, "It's this way. Poor Kerry moved out a few days ago. She had some family issues."

"Yes, you said that on the phone. Is she a good friend of yours?" I asked, making polite conversation."

It turned out the house was arranged over many floors, and soon we were climbing the second staircase.

"Not really, we just met like this, sharing a house, but I liked her. I'm sorry, I know we should have emptied out the room, but we've already dumped stuff in here. You know how tempting it is to hide crap and shut the door."

We walked through the bedroom door. I noticed it had a sturdy lock and key. Something that should've reassured me that my stuff would be safe, but only reminded me that I'd be living among strangers.

"Oh, there's not that much stuff in here. Don't worry about it." There were a few empty boxes, three suitcases, and a pile of shoes. Nevertheless, those few items took up most of the space; it was less than half of the size of my current room.

"All the bedrooms are about the same size, and the good thing for you, if you move in, is that your room is next to the bathroom."

Ominously, I noticed she said, "the bathroom," not "a bathroom."

"How many bathrooms are there?"

"Only one has a shower, that's the bathroom just next to here." She pointed to the bedroom wall. "There is one other, downstairs, that's just a toilet, no bath or shower."

One shower! Two toilets.

So, from this room, it would be a short hop to the communal facilities along with the convenience of hearing everyone else using them. Either the best or the worst room in the house, depending on how you measured it.

I wandered to the closet and opened the door. It appeared sturdy, clean, and well designed. "And how many people live here?"

"Three girls at the moment, you'd make four. They're all reasonably sized rooms with queen beds, much the same as this. Of course, any night a couple of us might have fellas over, you know. We're broadminded girls here. You can bring home a different guy every week or as many guys as you like." She raised an eyebrow. "Unless you're into girls, of course, which is fine too. What you do is your own business. Just keep the hallway clear in case there's a fire alarm. That's our only rule."

Four or six or more of us standing in line waiting for the one shower in the house. Oh. My. God.

Hopefully, I hid my horror at the predicament. It would've been rude not to because Elisha seemed nice and totally oblivious.

She continued chattering away. "You'll never need to feel lonely or unsafe, for that matter. It seems like there's always someone here, day and night. And if you ever need a man for anything or a bit of muscle, then my brothers live next door. They won't mind you calling on them."

"I'm living with guys right now." Before I drew breath in to say more, Elisha was talking again. I was beginning to suspect Elisha was more of a talker than a listener.

"Ha, yeah. I understand why you want to move now. Share with girlfriends and not a house full of men." She nodded in sympathy.

"They're not just any men." I sounded kind of defensive, which was how I felt about my men. "They're my stepbrothers."

Her eyes lit up. "Stepbrothers? That's interesting. So do you want to move home to carve out your own life away from your family?" She asked a question but didn't seem to want an answer. She nodded toward the wall. "You and I have so much

TRIPLET TIME 115

in common. The boys next door, they're my stepbrothers too. And they're twins."

"No! You have got to be joking! That's an amazing coincidence and for more reasons than you realize." As we discussed the coincidences in our lives, the conversation was dangerously close to spiraling into one-upmanship. "My stepbrothers are triplets."

Her eyes widened. "I really should ask this, um..."

"Obviously, you can't leave it there, Elisha; you've gotta tell me what you're thinking."

"As I've started dating a guy, I probably shouldn't ask, but are your triplet stepbrothers hot?"

"Oh." I let out a little scream and giggled. I hadn't expected that. "You first, are yours? Wait. They must be, or you wouldn't have asked."

"Look, let me show you the rest of the house, and we'll talk as we go." She stepped outside the small room.

"And you'll tell me?" I followed her out of the room and walked passed her to stand in the open doorway to the bathroom. It wasn't massive or luxurious, but it was clean and adequate. It took seconds for me to take it all in and step back out. "Well, are they hot?"

"Yes, I'll tell you, and yes, they're hot. I guess so, as they seem to have an entourage of girls around them at all times. And I've found myself surprisingly popular when girls find out they're my brothers. Just using me as a way to get an introduction, you know."

Did she sound jealous of all these girls her brothers dated, or was I projecting my issues about my stepbrothers?

"I can't blame the women attracted to good looking twins, after all. I've started dating one of their friends. My boyfriend, Darren, is also a twin. Not all twins look the same, of course, but when they do, and you're dating one of them… well, it quite catches my breath to see there are two who look the same."

"I can imagine." I could do more than imagine. The physical attraction and confusion I felt toward all three of my stepbrothers gave me some insight. But at least Elisha was legitimately dating one guy who was not even vaguely part of her family.

"Your turn, now Sophie," Elisha said over her shoulder as she led us back down the stairs.

"Yes, they're definitely hot."

"So you get a stream of girls staying over. I can see why you want to move out."

"No, actually, they don't." I realized that sounded weird. "I mean, they're not monks, but they're all working really hard. I think they probably did all the playing last year and the year before."

And I completely did not want to think about it. Not them with girls before me or after I moved out, Not any of them. We'd arrived in the kitchen, and I'd accepted Elisha's offer of a drink. The room certainly tempted me even though everything about this place was not as good as where I was living now. But I enjoyed talking to Elisha. Well, mostly listening.

"So the room is free right now. We'll get the pile of shoes removed. You can move in today as far as I'm concerned, and the other girls will be fine. I'll vouch for you. You'll fit in here. You just need to fill in all the paperwork and get checked out.

It's all managed by the student accommodation office. It should only take a couple of days."

CHAPTER FOURTEEN
CARL

The pleasant smell of food in the apartment made my stomach rumble when I arrived home, but there was no obvious sign of Sophie. It was her turn to cook, and she apparently had the job underway. She could've gone out, or she could've been in her room, where I didn't like to intrude as she had her door shut.

I went into my bedroom to relax a while, leaving my door open. That was how we did things. If anyone was home or when my brothers arrived back they could stick their heads in through my open doorway and say hello.

As brothers, we were used to walking in and out of each other's rooms, only shutting the door when privacy was required. A closed door more or less guaranteed no interruptions unless there was a fire.

The apartment was spacious enough to live an entire life in one room. Our bedrooms felt like our unique private domains, and they weren't so small that we'd go stir crazy in them.

Sophie's door was always closed. She was a girl, of course, hadn't grown up with us, and liked her privacy.

I kicked my shoes off and laid on the bed to browse social media and relax for a little while.

Sure enough, it wasn't too long before I heard the door open and voices. Adam and Ben arrived together. They called out greetings, and I replied as they both disappeared straight into their rooms to dump bags, change clothes, shower, or whatever.

I decided it was time to traipse through to the kitchen and investigate the smell more thoroughly as I'd only popped my head into the communal area earlier for long enough to see there was nobody there.

In the kitchen, two pots sat on the stove with the heat turned off. The contents were still warm. They had obviously been freshly cooked and were the source of the lovely aroma. As I moved toward the pans to investigate, I noticed a note sitting on the countertop.

When I picked it up and started to read, I heard footsteps coming toward me. I looked up as Ben entered the room.

"What's for dinner?" he asked, still approaching, looking at me, and then down at the slip of paper in my hand. "What've you got there?"

Before I answered either question, Adam had joined us. "Is it nearly ready? It smells nice."

I didn't have answers. Instead, I looked again at the notes. "It's Sophie's turn to cook, and she's left us a note." And I began to read it. "Hi guys, help yourselves to dinner. I've gone out for the evening, staying over at Nathan's, so don't worry about me. See you soon."

"Who the fuck is Nathan?" Adam didn't look at all happy.

"Her pal at college. And I don't know if he's more to her than that." My tone sounded as grim as I felt, and that was pretty damn grim.

"More than that. What do you mean?" Adam's tone said he was tuned to the channel my thoughts were on.

"Well, she talks about him a lot," I replied. My whole body tensed up with each word. "He seems to be one of her closest friends, and I don't know whether she has a crush on him, but I met him today."

I went on to tell the guys about what happened at school. How surprised she was to see me and not surprised in a delighted way, but not at all happy. I recounted our conversation, as best as I remembered it. And I told them how she bolted at the end of the class, so I had no chance to talk to her further.

"I don't understand why you never told her you do that nude modeling gig. You had plenty of opportunities." Ben pulled his phone out of his pocket and placed in on the dining table while he spoke. "Especially when we joked about it so much after she told us she'd be sketching nudes." He pulled out a chair and sat down at the table.

"It's art. Life modeling. You make it sound smutty. And I don't know why I didn't tell her either. But that's how it went, and it seriously backfired. It looks like she's avoiding me," I replied.

"Or all of us. She has a reason to avoid all of us." Adam looked despondent. "I wonder if this my fault?" He pulled a chair out from the table and sat down near Ben.

"Why? What did you do?" Ben asked.

"It turned out the romantic dinner suggestion worked well. Better than expected, actually, and one thing led to another." Adam glanced at me. I'd kind of seen the evidence and put it together. "We got extra friendly on the sofa and had some fun."

Ben blinked and blinked again. "I want to say, no way and good for you, both at the same time."

Adam didn't look as smug as he might have done under different circumstances. "Stick with 'no fucking way, jackass' because she ain't here now, and I haven't heard anything from her all day, so it looks like I screwed up."

It seemed as if I was doing dinner by default because I was closest, but I made no move to start. "Looks like we all did," I mumbled.

"How did it end with you and Sophie?" Ben asked.

"You two came home. We slept apart. I sent a few flirty texts last night. She responded. She seemed okay with it. But perhaps she wasn't, judging by the way she reacted to you, Carl. And I haven't heard anything from her today."

"It was only a couple of nights ago she was with me. She seemed perfectly happy about the whole thing at the time, and then the next day, she ran away from me in the morning, and by nighttime, she's making out with you."

"And today in the art class she told me she thought we were all, um, handsome, I think that was the word she used."

Chewing on his lip, Ben nodded. "Bros, it seems to me she really must like us." He waved a hand around, indicating all three of us. "Or else she wouldn't mess about with two of us, one night after another, and then freak out when she sees Carl's junk. She as good as told Carl she likes us. I guess she might be freaking out because there's three of us, and she thinks she has to choose." He looked at his phone on the table and tapped the screen.

We all remained still and silent for a while, each man lost in his thoughts.

"Either that or she can't believe her good luck," Ben said suddenly. "Because we're awesome."

Trust Ben to break the tension. We all laughed a little.

"She might be avoiding us because she's worried we'll get jealous or something." Adam looked at Ben as he spoke.

"You've got a point." I turned the heat on under the pans, took the lids off, and stirred the food. "You know guys, we've talked among ourselves, but maybe we need to be honest with Sophie and tell her straight that we all like her."

"Agreed," said Ben. "It's all very well trying to seduce her, and she obviously does like us, but if she likes all three of us, maybe that's what worrying her."

"So, what's this Nathan guy like?" Adam asked.

"I've met him when I dropped her at school a few times," said Ben. "He looks like a skinny young art student. A few years younger than us. What more is there to say? I'm not really into dudes, so I've never paid much attention."

"It doesn't matter what we think of him. She likes him." I got the plates ready on the countertop. The food wasn't cold to start with, so reheating wouldn't take long.

"I've never met the dude, but I can't help feeling I don't like him. I guess he's our competition, and I hope he keeps his hands off our Sophie." Grim Adam was back in the room.

I felt myself nodding in agreement; I knew exactly what Adam meant. "Look, she's just out for the night. Maybe they've gone to see a band or a movie or something. It's not as if she's moved out. She hasn't dumped us to move in with him."

What a terrible thought. We all remained quiet for a while after that. I didn't know what my brothers were thinking, but I was stuck on how horrible it would be if she moved out. I started to dish up.

Adam stood up and got the cutlery. "What if she did decide to leave? That would be awful."

I took the three full plates to the table. "I've liked having her here."

It was as if she completed something that had been missing in recent years.

CHAPTER FIFTEEN
SOPHIE

I met Nathan a short distance from the next viewing appointment, and as we were a little early, I had time to tell him about the house I looked at earlier. "I quite liked it. It wasn't my dream home, but I could live there."

"Even with only one shower to for everyone to share, giving you a chance of a taste of how the other half lives?"

"I didn't come from a rich family, Nathan," I protested. "I know how the other half lives. My mom had only married Mr. Cooper less than a year ago. And being very religious and traditional, she didn't live with him beforehand. She's old-fashioned that way. Mom was a hard-working single mother for years after Dad died; big luxurious homes and spare money is all new to me."

"Fine. Still, if I lived in a big luxury apartment, I'm not sure I'd be eager to step down from having a private bathroom to slumming it."

"I don't want to either. But I can't face living with the boys."

We were outside the next place. It was a shared apartment.

"I've been thinking about that." He came to a halt, and I realized we were standing outside the building. "We'll talk after."

We didn't say much as we looked at my new prospective home. The lady who showed us around was about my age, and unlike Elisha, she wasn't chatty. Nathan came in to check the place out with me.

"This is my friend, Nathan," I said. And when she eyed him coldly I added, "He's not my boyfriend, just a friend." Just in case she thought he'd be staying over every night.

"I didn't think he was," she replied. I wondered if she was referring to the fact that he didn't look like he'd be any woman's boyfriend. He was so flamboyant that most people assumed he was gay, which he was, of course.

I'd only be living with this one woman, and she wasn't nearly as friendly as Elisha. At least I'd only share a bathroom and the communal area with one person instead of four strangers plus all of their boyfriends.

I would have more space, quiet, and privacy in this apartment, but Elisha's house might offer more fun, it was closer to college and in an altogether nicer part of Arlington. The thought of walking through the streets after dark in this area didn't appeal, and driving a car everywhere didn't appeal either.

This apartment had many positive features.

I didn't make a firm commitment there and then. I had to weigh up the pros and cons. She said someone else was coming to see the room the next day, that might have been a bluff, and I wasn't going to be pressured into making a big decision on the spot.

We agreed to talk on the phone the next day when I'd let her know one way or the other. And, of course, she might reject me too. Because in this apartment, she had the last word.

After ten minutes and no offer of a drink, we were on our way to Nathan's home.

"So, what's your plan?" he asked.

"I don't know. I do need to think it over. But my gut reaction is to go with the other place. I'm going to stay at your place tonight and toss a coin in the morning over which room to take. I'll sort it out from there."

"So, you're dead set on moving out?"

"Didn't we have this conversation already? Yes, I'm moving out. It's for the best. In fact, I don't think I've much choice, not after seeing all of their dicks over the course of three days."

"It'll take a few days for them to check you out, transfer money, sort out contracts. You can stay at my place while that's happening if you want to."

"Thanks, Nathan, you're a pal. If you didn't offer, I was going to invite myself anyway."

"I had a funny feeling about that."

We both giggled.

"Thing is, I just can't face them."

Nathan sighed. "I gave Carl my number. I'm still hoping he'll do some modeling for me. He seemed enthusiastic at the time, I thought. You could come along too and sketch him. It'll add to your portfolio, and we can double up on studio time and split the model fee. Hell, he might even give us a friends and family discount. It's a total win-win. What do you say?"

When he'd started talking about Carl modeling, I thought he was serious. I groaned as he went on, and I realized he was winding me up.

"That's a no?" He laughed, and I slipped my arm through his.

"I say you are the devil, Nathan. And I don't know why I'm friends with you. I do not want to spend any more time in a room with those naked men."

"Oh, sweetie, I don't know how you can possibly say that."

The next day I still hadn't one hundred percent decided which room to accept. They both had positive and negative sides to consider. And neither of them was as good an option as living with my stepbrothers.

Damn it, if only it weren't for the fact of them being my stepbrothers or that I liked every single one of them.

The next day, I turned up outside the accommodation office, ready to toss a coin; I didn't know which to choose. Not just heads or tails. The house with many people to share the bathroom or the apartment with one person. But whether to move away from the three boys or stay with them.

Nathan had given me quite a talk.

He was shocked when I first told him I was working my way through my stepbrothers, but when he'd had time to let the idea sink in, he came out with a very modern perspective on things.

Let's say, he suggested tapping into bohemian art history and follow the examples of many twentieth-century artists who experimented with alternative relationships. Failing that, I should have a second stab at a platonic friendship with them because they were good guys, and they were family.

TRIPLET TIME

While pacing up and down along the corridor outside the accommodation office, I thought about how I'd always had Mom around to help with the big things in life. Moving away from home was a significant decision to make on my own without discussing it with my mom. I'd never done anything like this before, but it wasn't as if I could just phone her and admit to what had happened with the guys.

What would they think of me leaving the triplets? I felt guilty about doing something on my own that would affect the whole family. And I didn't have long to procrastinate before my next class.

Both mom and the boys would be suspicious of me moving out without a word to any of them. If I went through with this, without talking it through with them first, it might devastate our family dynamics.

I thought I should at least talk to Mom before taking action. If I explained I'd met some nice girls and they suggested I move in with them, that wouldn't be a complete lie. The idea of sharing with some girls might seem appealing and a credible excuse for my sudden change of address, I figured.

But even I didn't buy it.

Why would I move out?

Before getting too intimately acquainted with them all, I'd enjoyed living with the guys, and I loved the luxuriousness of the apartment. The place was kept ridiculously neat and clean. I like how we shared the chores, eating together, and hanging out after dinner. Walking to college each day with one of the guys, usually Ben, was also a nice thing to do.

And my mom would worry about my safety if I moved out. That was no small concern. She liked the idea that I was with the boys and was comforted by the idea that they looked after me. And to be fair, I did feel safe and cared for.

After one night apart from them all, I was missing them already.

I had classes to attend and research to do, so I decided to put off the accommodation office and the big decision until I was able to give it more consideration after all.

There was no chance of running into the guys while I was at college. Their business courses were at a different location. However, even though Nathan offered hospitality, I couldn't avoid our apartment. If for no other reason than to change my clothes, I had to go home at some time that day.

When I arrived home, all the guys were there. I heard their voices, all of them talking over each other and sounding excited.

I closed the main door as quietly as possible. There was a chance they didn't hear me come home over their chatter. Not that I could completely avoid them, but I went directly into my room and closed the door. My heartbeat already raced. I felt nervous about facing each of them individually and together.

My stomach churned. I felt physically ill.

The huge urge to simply run away and never face them and never tell them I was leaving loomed great and almost overwhelmed me.

Yet I'd avoided the accommodation office. I hadn't signed anything, no one had done a check on me, and I'd paid no deposit. I'd avoided taking that step toward committing to a new home.

I sorted out a bag of clean clothes and stuff I might need to allow me two clear nights out at Nathan's place. All the while I packed a bag, I also wondered how I'd face the guys and what I'd say.

The decision was made easy when I heard a knock at my door.

"Sophie, dinner is ready." They must've heard me arrive home. "Sophie, it's Ben."

"I heard, Ben. Thanks, I'll be out in a minute," I replied.

"Can I speak to you?"

I pushed open the door.

"Sophie, I just want two minutes." He glanced toward the kitchen and back at me. "Can I come in, please?"

I opened the door wider, and my eyes skimmed the room as I did so.

The boys didn't usually enter my room. My room was always such a mess compared to theirs and the rest of the house, so I preferred to keep my door closed and visitors out. Fortunately, the constant mess meant it wasn't obvious that I was sorting through stuff and packing an overnight bag.

As my room remained private, he wouldn't know whether it looked different from usual.

"What's the matter?" As I asked, the irony was he could be asking me the same thing. But he knocked on my door, so I got to ask the questions.

"They are waiting for dinner. I just needed to tell you, one-to-one, that I like you a lot, Sophie. I'd love there to be something between us, and I understand you don't want that, so I want you to know I won't make life uncomfortable for you. I'm here if you change your mind, but don't let what happened between us stop you from dating my brothers. I'm still here for you as a roommate and a brother if we're not going to be more than that."

I sat down on the edge of my bed before my legs gave way beneath me. I wasn't expecting him to say any of that.

"I just thought you should know it wouldn't create any bad feelings between us if you started seeing either of my brothers or both of my brothers." He turned back toward the door as if to leave.

Did I hear him correctly? "Both of your brothers?"

"Pardon?" he said.

"I'm hardly going to date both of your brothers at the same time."

"They'd like it if you did. We'd all like to date you, Sophie."

Whatever the hell he had in mind, I didn't discover because he promptly left the room.

CHAPTER SIXTEEN
SOPHIE

I closed the door behind me and followed Ben out of my room and along the hallway.

Carl and Adam were sitting at the table, engaged in conversation.

I went and sat at the table in my usual seat. Would I have a usual place if I lived in another home?

Ben walked directly to the oven and stood next to it. I realized the food wasn't ready; he'd probably just put it in as it was Ben's night to cook. In my next home, would we have communal meals and a cooking schedule?

Ben's night could be renamed pizza night. Pizzas didn't take long to cook, which was why Ben didn't show any intentions of lingering in my room for a lengthy discussion, or we'd be having burnt offerings.

"I'm glad you're here tonight," said Adam.

Only then did it occur to me that after what we did, he probably felt rejected, just as Ben did. I felt guilty for not returning more of his texts.

Carl nodded. "We missed you yesterday, but thanks for the lovely food. You obviously cooked before you went out."

I shrugged. "No problem."

"I'm sorry about yesterday. I hope you don't feel you have to avoid me because of that. Next time I'm planning to take my clothes off in public, I'll let you know."

Lost for words, I shrugged again. I had no right to make Carl feel bad about his legitimate part-time job.

"I may as well tell you if I ever get a chance to be in a Spencer Tunick installation, I'll be there. With no clothes whatsoever," Carl declared gleefully.

I laughed.

Adam tilted his head and blinked.

"Spencer Tunick is famous for his photographs of large gatherings of nude people in iconic public places," I explained.

"You'd know his work if you saw it. In some of it, the people are colored blue," Carl said.

I wondered why he thought the blue people detail was the one thing worth mentioning, rather than any of the famous images and locations. The triplets had a history together, and I was still on the outside.

Adam picked up his phone. "Tunick?" he said as he tapped on the screen. He remained silent as he read or looked at the art, I couldn't tell which.

"I couldn't imagine gathering with hundreds of naked people," I said to Carl.

"So when I do, you'll have to come along and hold my clothes." His eyes sparkled with humor.

"I will. It'd be cool to be a part of creating something like that," I agreed and began to wonder when and where the next opportunity would be.

"Thousands gather for those things. I can't believe I'm saying this, but I'd do it too." Adam looked up from the phone and smiled. "It seems a bit like being in a flash mob."

"Yes, but with less dancing and fewer clothes and completely legal." Tuned into my artist's brain, I couldn't help thinking aloud. "The three of you together, looking so alike but different. Um, the right artist could do beautiful things with your bodies."

Carl nodded. We understood each other.

"You could be the artist who does beautiful things with our bodies if you want, Sophie." Adam stared intently across the table at me, and I wasn't sure whether he meant something artist or if it was only my mind that went to the gutter.

I gulped.

"I'm sorry, Sophie, about the night before. If I went too far, we don't have to do anything like that again unless you want to, in which case I'd be all for it."

My cheeks flushed. That was the sort of conversation I'd expect to have in private, not in front of an audience. Carl watched me, and when I glanced up at Ben, he leaned across the countertop.

"Two minutes left on the timer," Ben said.

Thank you for saving me, I thought. Adam still looked as if he wanted an answer.

"I don't have to forgive you for anything. You don't need to say sorry, you've done nothing wrong."

"Great. So we're all friends again. No bad feeling. No holding grudges," said Carl.

I couldn't help smiling too. I'd dreaded how awkward this situation might become, but it was turning out fine. I'd mistreated each one of these guys. Not terribly, but they deserved better.

Ben suddenly appeared beside me, holding a plate of olives and sun-dried tomatoes, which he placed in the center of the table. He was keeping up with the conversation too.

"I owe you guys apologies all around, I think. I may not have been polite and considerate. I'll try to do better in the future."

Adam responded, "You don't need to worry. I won't hold a grudge against you. I won't hold anything against you that you don't want. And that's a promise. I'm totally up for holding things close if you want to."

Adam's innuendo should have made me blush, but we were all so busy laughing, except Ben, who was whooping. The guys were over the top and funny. And I knew everything was back to normal.

I loved these guys and their sense of humor. Their openness with each other amazed me.

It felt as if it were my turn to say something again; I looked down at my fingers that fidgeted on the table.

"I like you all. I couldn't possibly choose between you and date one of you. If that's what you're asking, which is perhaps not what you meant. If you're offering friends with benefits... no." I shook my head. If they didn't want to date me and this was a casual encounter they were talking about, then I was afraid I embarrassed myself. I regretted saying anything at all.

Carl coughed and ran his fingers through his hair. "I've really enjoyed hanging out with you since you moved in, and I would definitely like us to date if you would be willing."

For a moment, it felt as if I was sucked into a void that contained just Carl and myself, and no one else was there. Not the other brothers. Not the room. Not the rest of the city. That lasted just long enough for me to say nothing.

Adam broke the spell. "You and Carl would make a great couple, but don't decide right now, not until you've considered the other options. There may be a few other offers. I happen to know at least one or two other guys who'd like to date you." A flirty smile flickered across his face, which made me grin.

This evening was getting to be fun. And interesting.

Before anyone said anything else, a piercing beeping sound came from Ben's direction. "Hold that thought; we're not finished yet. Pizza is done," he announced as he pulled open the oven door.

He brought two huge pizzas, cut into slices, to the table along with garlic bread and a bowl of salad. Catering wasn't Ben's thing, but he always fed us well, nevertheless. He sat down with us.

Presented with colorful food and a delicious aroma made me realize how hungry I was. The guys must have felt the same. For a few minutes, we focused on the food rather than the conversation.

After we'd all eaten our first slice and were some way into the second, Ben said, "Now is no time to change the subject, Sophie. The truth is we'd all like to date you."

I looked around the table at each of their faces.

They were all looking at me. Each man nodded when we made eye contact.

"We're serious about a relationship," Carl said.

"Why doesn't it surprise me that you three seem to have discussed this?" I rubbed my arm and then my face. "Are you three asking if I want to choose one of you? I like you all, and this is really awkward."

Adam bit into his pizza and watched me.

Ben bit his lip.

Carl placed his hand down flat on the table. "No, that's not what we're saying at all. I mean, if you do want to date one of us, it will be fine. We'd like you to think about having a relationship with all of us. I know it's unusual, but people do that kind of thing, and we'd like to try it with you."

I couldn't help but giggle. What does a girl say to something like that?

"Now, everyone, please eat the food before it gets cold. I went to a lot of trouble preparing this."

As he so often did, Ben lightened the mood and saved me from the pressure to give an immediate answer.

We all looked down at the food on our plates and picked up slices of pizza.

"And it is delicious. Thanks," Carl said.

When the three guys were both sweet and sexy, what girl wouldn't be tempted to turn our dinner arrangement into something more romantic?

They'd offered me all my Christmases at once. From being a boring girl from a small town, I'd become somebody three hot guys all wanted at the same time.

And instead of having to choose between them, they were suggesting the most outrageous thing of all. How could that even work?

I pulled out my phone to send a text to Nathan. Whatever happened, I didn't need to run away that night, far from it. I had to stay with the triplets and uncover the full extent of their intentions.

CHAPTER SEVENTEEN
BEN

As far as I was concerned, we'd laid our cards on the table. If Sophie wanted to pick any or all of them up, the ball was firmly in her court.

Having thought I was close, I'd been rejected once. She knew I was still interested, and I wasn't about to push it. After all, we were still friends, and we lived in the same apartment. I didn't want her to freak out and think I turned into some pushy housemate who she needed to avoid.

We'd all been getting along perfectly well before any of us had made physical contact. There was no reason to start acting weird and no reason for our behavior to change.

Things were a little weird, no matter how much I tried to pretend they weren't.

Much as I'd shared everything with my brothers, I'd never actually shared a woman with them.

We'd never shared a girlfriend or a one-night stand.

Things were different with Sophie; for one thing, I'd never felt this way about a woman before. Physical attractions and lust, I'd had those feelings. But after the friendship I'd built up with Sophie, the way I felt about her was something new.

I had all these emotions churning inside.

The past few days when I hadn't seen her, I'd missed her terribly. And I couldn't stop thinking about her.

This wasn't the sort of thing I'd generally talk about. I'd never tell my friends. My brothers were different. And I'd confessed how her rejection hurt as bad as real physical pain.

Of course, they laughed, joked, and ribbed me about it, then admitted they felt much the same way about her.

We discussed sharing Sophie, and there were things we hadn't discussed. But those things wouldn't matter if Sophie wasn't interested. We were going to take our lead from her.

After we'd finished eating dinner, Adam made some comment about a dessert that set him and Sophie sniggering. Even Carl started to laugh. I suspected there was a private joke, and I wasn't in on it.

They all went and sat on the sofa in front of the TV, Sophie in the middle, my brothers either side of her. Adam had his arm casually draped over the back of the seat behind Sophie. I rolled my eyes; his behavior was so corny.

After clearing the plates from the table, I fished in the freezer for multiple tubs of ice cream, strawberry, vanilla, and chocolate. I'd serve them a triple delight. I grated some chocolate over it and topped it with crumbled cookies.

I took the ice cream to them to eat in front of the TV, so Adam had to take his arm from behind Sophie's head. I sat down in a chair to eat my own.

The TV was on as background entertainment. None of us wanted to watch it, I was sure. Some ridiculous game-show distracted us from the things we wanted to talk about. Tucking into bowls of ice cream seemed to relieve the tension. We didn't have to speak about anything, and it gave us something to focus our attention on and do with our hands. We didn't have to talk, but we made comments about the sweet and delicious dessert.

The sound of spoons clinking against the ceramic bowls was the only sound apart from the TV for a couple of minutes, and then Sophie said, "I'm sorry about biting your head off over the modeling. I feel guilty about that. I had no right to do that. It wouldn't have been a problem if it had been anyone else, so it shouldn't have been a problem that I knew you."

"No worries. I should've told you." Carl dropped his spoon into his bowl and placed the empty bowl on the table.

"Yeah, well, forget it. I am curious, though, how you got into being a model at my college when you don't even go to the same school?"

"Many of my photography classes were at your campus last year, actually. But as for the life class modeling, your art school was casting a wider net than just among their own students. I saw a notice on the board a few years ago when we first started college. Needless to say, a lot of the guys thought it a hilarious joke. A few of them went through with it once. I think the drop out rate can be high."

Sophie giggled. "I can imagine. It did look like a pretty boring job."

Quite a few of the guys who did it did so only once.

"Exactly. I don't do it often."

"Nathan gave you his number; he's specializing in the male body. Are you going to contact him? I want you to know that I don't mind if you do. Not that you need my permission."

She must have sensed some reaction to her comment, even though we all had deadpan expressions.

"What's the matter with you all?" She looked around. "Have you got a problem with Nathan because he is gay?"

Carl let out the biggest laugh, soon followed by the rest of us.

"What did I say? What's so funny?"

"Nathan is gay," Carl said but could manage nothing more because he was laughing so hard.

"What's funny about being gay? Am I living with a bunch of homophobes, and I didn't know it?"

"It's not that," I said. "We thought he was our competition, and you might be into him."

Sophie grinned and chuckled.

"We didn't know he was gay." I looked at Carl. "No wonder he'd like to see more of you with your clothes off."

"How could you think he was anything other?" Sophie broke into a full belly laugh. "Just for that slur on his good name, all three of you should volunteer your naked bodies to his art." She apparently thought that was very funny, and we all laughed too.

"In my defense, I don't mind one bit stripping off for a gay dude," said Carl, when we quietened down. "Sophie, you did say something interesting while biting my head off."

"Did I?"

She looked as curious as I was.

"Yes. Something about you liking all of us." Carl gestured around the room as he brought us back to the subject that must have been on everyone's mind.

Poor Sophie's face went red, and she took another mouthful of ice cream.

Adam shifted a little at his end of the seat to direct his attention toward her rather than the TV screen.

"Well, of course," Sophie began, "if a woman is attracted to any one of you, she's going to feel the same way about all three of you because you look alike."

"Do we now?" I laughed at her, stating the obvious, and then the others joined in.

"You know what I mean," Sophie protested. "And it's not just about looks. You're all so lovely. I wouldn't want to have to choose between you."

"And you don't, Sophie. You don't have to choose between us. You can choose to have us all," Carl said in such a matter-of-fact way that I wanted to whisper in his ear a word about wooing and romance. The irony was he was supposedly the more artistic of the three of us.

"You guys are really serious, aren't you? Serious and persistent. It's a big decision. I'll have to give it some thought."

Sitting in a single armchair, I felt so far away. I longed to touch her and reconnect the way we had just a few nights ago. I wanted to tell her how beautiful she looked and show her how much I desired her because she was beautiful on the outside as well as the inside.

She didn't say *no* outright, and the underlying tension in the room didn't ease. If anything, she'd raised our hopes. The atmosphere felt charged with sexual energy. The tension in the room was so palpable it couldn't have only been me. I was sure all three of them wanted to clarify our relationship as much as I did.

Taking Adam's bowl out of his hand, Sophie placed both of their bowls on the table and cuddled up to Adam's side. His arm had finally made it and was draped over her shoulder.

My brothers and I wanted to move things forward with Sophie and make her feel good.

We'd tried to tell her, but I'm not sure she got it.

I wasn't sure she really understood we were talking about her having three relationships, one with each of us. We already had a strong bond as brothers, and nothing was going to break that. Sharing the same woman, being in love with the same woman, it made so much sense.

Something different than most other people had. Not something you see on television, but something that would work for us.

Kicking my shoes off to get more comfortable, I noticed everybody still had their shoes on.

"How are your feet, Sophie?"

She looked at me and blinked rapidly with surprise. The question was a bit out of the blue.

"Fine. Why?"

I leaned forward to put my empty dessert bowl on the table. "All that walking to and from college. I thought you might like a foot massage."

She raised her feet slightly and wound the ankles in two opposite circular motions. "If you're offering, that sounds great."

Without delay, I fell to my knees at her feet and removed her shoes. I held her feet in my hands. I knew enough about foot massage that a firm grip was required to avoid tickling her. I placed both feet on my lap and began to work on one.

After pushing her toes back until they were fully flexed, I rubbed my palm along the undercarriage of her foot.

She hummed. "That feels really good. I've never had a foot massage before."

We wanted to give her many things she'd never had before. She had no idea.

Using the fingers and knuckles of clenched fists, I pushed into the fleshy parts of her foot, applying the greatest pressure to her heel. My fingertips and the palms of my hand worked over the bony parts. I carefully rested the foot down before doing the same to the other.

Sophie reminded me of a cat lying on a sofa purring with delight as it was stroked by the owner.

Carl and Adam watched with some interest.

"My feet ache a little," Carl mumbled.

"I'm not into big boy's feet," I replied. In my hands, Sophie's feet were so small, smooth, and delicate.

Sophie took hold of Carl's hand and threaded her fingers through his. I didn't imagine it; it was definitely her who took the initiative there. She reached out to him.

Holding hands with Carl, leaning against Adam and with me at her feet, her body language suggested she was quite amenable to the three of us.

"It's not just a foot massage. I've never had a massage at all. In fact, there are many things I haven't experienced." Sophie blushed, and I wondered what was going through her mind. Something dirty, judging by the expression on her face.

I couldn't help getting a little hotter myself as I thought about things we hadn't done together in the bedroom. Not that the others knew. I'd never tell my bros the details. I couldn't speak, but my brothers did.

"I'm sure we can help you out with your experiences. We can certainly do massage," said Carl.

"Is there anything else you've got in mind?" Adam said.

Judging by the way her face had gone even redder, there was something else she was considering, and it may well have been dirty. I loved this girl.

She bit her bottom lip and offered no more information.

"You know, a massage would feel so much better if you were lying down completely flat." I squeezed up above her ankle, hinting at the possibility. "If you weren't wearing jeans, I could do your calf muscles as well."

"Laying flat. Are you suggesting like on a bed?"

CHAPTER EIGHTEEN
SOPHIE

Through the course of that stressful, unhappy day, I would never have envisioned its ending would involve Carl leading me by the hand to his bedroom, Adam and Ben following close behind.

"I need to grab a shower," Adam said. "I'll join you in a minute."

I heard Ben say, "And me."

"I need one, too." I released Carl's hand and stepped toward my room, but Carl kept a firm grip on me.

"Mine's the biggest," Carl boasted. "And I'm talking about bathrooms. So come and share with me and save on water."

The invitation for shower sharing was clearly only aimed at me, and I didn't resist the gentle pull in the direction of Carl's room.

I glanced behind. Ben had already disappeared into his room.

Adam winked at me as he walked past to his own.

On the opposite side of the corridor to our three bedrooms, Carl occupied the master suite. For that reason, we all agreed he had the best space for the six-handed massage that they were offering.

Once we stepped into his room, and with the door still open, he pulled me into a warm embrace. Our faces were drawn together, our mouths finding each other.

Over the few weeks we'd lived together, Carl had become my best friend in the city. He was fun to hang out with, and we had a lot of interests in common. I now discovered he was also a fantastic kisser.

He held me firmly against him. My body yielded and molded to fit with his while his tongue slipped through my open lips and into my mouth.

I never expected to kiss my best friend. I wasn't prepared for how good it felt or how much my whole body would hum with desire when he held me like this.

As if we were in tune and chemistry meant us to be together in this way.

Somehow he undressed me while we kissed.

My mind remained more focused on the pleasurable contact, the taste and smell of his skin, so I hardly noticed my clothes slipping away. I should have felt self-conscious as he removed my clothes, especially with his bedroom door still open. But there was no requirement for privacy.

Suddenly aware of my near nudity, I rolled my hip as he slipped his hands into the top of my panties to ease them down. How could I be self-conscious before him when we were fellow artists? I'd seen him naked, after all.

His hands cupped my bare ass cheeks as he pulled me towards him again, kissing me with a little more urgency. I could feel the hard erection through his clothes pushing against my bare stomach. I loved the feeling and that he was turned on like this.

Reluctantly, I pushed him away. "Shower," I whispered. My voice was a little hoarse.

He stepped back and grinned. "Come on," he said as he pulled his top over his head and strode toward his bathroom.

He'd reached the bathroom door before I could move. Naked, vulnerable, and excited, my brain didn't send the signal to my legs to move as it was too busy watching the excellent rear view of the topless man. I already knew he had fine muscle definition as a result of the art class. Now, I was getting a private showing, and his hands in front of him seemed to be undoing his fly.

As his pants started to slip down, I sucked in a deep breath.

He glanced over his shoulder at me. "Are you ready?"

Nodding, I walked to join him. "I am."

"I'll get the water going." He shed his pants and underwear in a swift blur of movement and disappeared into the bathroom.

It was massive. I'd glanced in his bathroom only once before when I'd had an initial tour of the house. The walk-in shower was itself the size of a small room, fully tiled and with multiple body jets. It was big enough for two; it could easily accommodate four.

When I walked into the room, the water was already cascading, but Carl was still fingering the remote control. All the bathrooms had remote control operated showers, but Carl's bathroom was by far the most impressive. I realized he wasn't changing the water setting but turning on the atmospheric mood lighting. A romantic red glow descended over the room.

He held out a hand, which I took in mine, and we stepped into the wet space together.

"It's so massive in here the other boys could have joined us too."

"I'm not going to worry that they didn't."

"I suppose the three of you are so big it would certainly seem rather crowded in here."

"Yes, and you might like it, but from my point of view, it would start to feel like having a shower after a sports match. You know, too many guys."

He squeezed shower gel on his hands from the pump dispenser, rubbed his hands together, and then stepped behind me. "I thought if you went for a shower in your room, you might have second thoughts and not reappear for the night."

"You're right; I'd probably have been overcome with nerves."

He smothered the shower gel over my shoulder blade and down my back. It felt great. "You're not too overcome with nerves now?"

"I'm in your shower, Carl. And naked. And your brothers are coming back in a minute to give me a massage. Yes, I'm very nervous."

He kissed the back of my neck, and his soapy hands slipped down my arms as he came closer to me. His breath and affectionate kisses were reassuring. His solid chest against my back felt strong and comforting. His erection, however, felt big and heavy and dominated my thoughts. Arousal unfurled deep and low within me.

Carl's long arms made it easy for him to reach right around me. He rubbed the coconut-scented liquid across my stomach.

His hands skirted the edge of my pubis before he moved up and over my breasts.

First, he cupped my breasts, one in each hand. Then he lightly brushed over them with his fingertips, pleasantly teasing. When he touched my nipples, it was as if he'd found the place to ignite my passion.

A wanton moan escaped me. "I need to wash."

And get a grip if I'm to survive tonight.

I stepped forward to reach for the shower gel, and Carl read my body language and released me. We both soaped ourselves up, and feeling cleaner, I turned to face him.

For the first time since we'd been in the shower, I looked at him. Close up, soaking wet, and coated in soapy suds, he looked gorgeous. I'd have to be crazy to reject this man. I'd be unlikely to find anyone who was both as wonderful and as sexy in just one package, with the possible exception of his brothers.

I reached up, laying my palms flat on his chest, and ran my soapy hands over his big hard muscles.

"Careful you don't slip." He moved the water over my shoulders, rinsing the remaining bubbles off. The soap all but washed away, leaving the lingering scent of coconut on our skin.

"It doesn't feel slippery underfoot."

"I'll check that out."

He got down on his knees in the shower in front of me. His hands slipped behind me and grasped my ass while he pressed his face against my pussy. His nose flicked from side to side against my clit two or three times.

Giggling, I inched my legs apart to allow him easier access.

Carl took advantage of the opportunity. His tongue swept up and down in long strokes as he lapped along my slit in a way that was gentle, experienced, and meant business.

When his tongue probed around my clit, I became weak at the knees; I swear it was his hands on my ass that held me upright. Nevertheless, I staggered backward until I had the tiled shower wall for additional support.

My new position, leaning against the wall, made it all so much easier. First, his tongue pushed into my wet entrance, quickly followed by a finger.

I gasped.

I wanted this and knew it was coming, but when it did, it felt better than ever I expected.

He slid in another finger, two, perhaps? I couldn't be sure.

He turned me on as I'd never imagined possible. Standing in the wet, humid atmosphere with him at my feet felt like nothing like I'd previously experienced.

The hot spray continued to cascade, hitting my stomach and his head and shoulders. It didn't put him off.

His tongue and fingers played me with such a light touch; it was somewhere between pleasure and torture.

I was moaning loudly with ecstasy but too turned on to stop or quieten down. I could come any second.

Leaning against the drenched wall tiles, I rested my hands on his sopping hair.

I wanted to get closer to him, to feel his skin against me and his face against mine. His cock in me. Coming in me.

Finding some self-control, I grasped his hair and forced his head back away from me. Having gained space to maneuver, I lowered to my knees in front of him. I smiled when we were again at eye level, the two of us on our knees in the shower. There had to be easier ways to do this.

He smiled back at me and licked his lips.

I moved forward to kiss him and grasped hold of his cock. It felt big in my hand, and I longed to feel it inside me.

I rubbed my cheek against his and whispered in his ear. "Carl, I want you to fuck me." Of all the three men in my life, it suddenly seemed clear that Carl should be my first; he should finally take my prized virginity.

"I will, when we get out. It's more comfortable on a bed."

He twisted his fingers, and they plunged deeper inside me. I let out a gasp.

"I can make you come other ways as well."

He could, and he was going to.

"I love feeling you so so wet and turned on."

I loved hearing him talk like this.

He increased the speed of his fingers thrusting into me. "I love having my fingers inside you. I can feel your channel clamping around me."

"Feels so good!" I shouted. He could feel me coming, and I didn't want to hold back any longer. I couldn't stop this.

Upon my knees and bucking as each wave of the climax hit, I shamelessly cried out and wrapped my arms around his shoulders for stability.

Mercilessly his fingers plundered.

"So good. So. Good. Yes!"

When the excitement subsided, I collapsed on to him for only a few seconds before I realized it wasn't a comfortable place to rest at all. I raised my head.

He stood up and offered his hand to help me up.

As I got to my feet, I noticed his brothers in the doorway. They both stared, wide-eyed and open-mouthed.

Ben had a white towel wrapped around his hips. It hung low and didn't conceal the massive bulge over which he held his hand.

In contrast, Adam had a towel slung over his shoulders, his erection in his hand, held out on display.

I still felt aroused and ready for more, and discovering that they'd watched only made me feel sexier. Seeing their evident approval and enjoyment of the display made things even better.

Carl turned the water off and wrapped me in a large fluffy towel. "You'll need to be very dry, as massaging damp skin doesn't work too well." He picked up another smaller towel and wrapped it around my head. I felt very exotic and pampered.

"I want you to fuck me, Carl," I said to him in a whisper but loud enough for them all to hear. "You must be the first man to fuck me."

CHAPTER NINETEEN
CARL

Every word and every sentence that she uttered seemed to make physical contact with my dick; she didn't even need to touch it. She stroked my libido with her arousal and promises of what was next.

When she told me I must be the first, my mind slipped between the two possible meanings. Either she wanted me to be the first man to enter her tonight, or something.

When I wrapped her in the towel, she curled up into my arms.

"Carl, please fuck me." She sounded almost pleading.

As I was desperate for her, it seemed as though she wanted me just as much, even though my brothers were right there with us.

They stepped aside, and Sophie and I passed through the doorway and went to my bed. She lay down, still wrapped in the damp towel, looking as beautiful as I'd ever seen her.

"Turn over," I whispered and guided her on to her stomach. I slipped the towel away and ran my hands down her back.

My brothers had heard her, of course.

"I want you to fuck me, Carl. You must be the first man to fuck me."

They stayed back at a respectful distance. I knew they wouldn't force themselves on her. A man has to feel wanted, and I sensed they were unsure of what to do.

"Do you want Adam and Ben to touch you, too?" I asked. As I said these words, it occurred to me how odd it was that it didn't seem strange to me. I wanted them with me, on the bed, enjoying her body. I hoped she wanted that too.

She looked up at them. "You guys offered a massage, are you ready?"

They both grinned.

Ben dropped the towel and walked around the bed to the far side. I slipped down to position myself between her knees, and Adam came alongside, too.

What followed was little like a massage. We touched her with our hands. Six hands stroked her skin, but that was where the similarity to any regular massage ended.

Along with my brothers, I covered every inch of her skin with tender kisses and gentle bites. At times our three hard cocks rubbed over her back and arms and legs, leaving trails of sticky precum in their wake. It was erotic and fun.

She sighed, whimpered, and moaned with pleasure, and her body rocked. Her thighs slowly relaxed, moving further and further apart. I could smell the delicious womanly scent calling to me; I wanted to bury my face there but held back to escalate her gratification. The longer we made her wait, the better it would feel. I saw her pink flesh lips, swollen and glistening wet with arousal.

TRIPLET TIME

The more we teased her, the higher her ass raised into the air. I didn't want it to cross over into a cruel game of turning her on and never meeting her needs. As if that would happen.

I slipped my hand between her legs, underneath her, to stroke her pussy for the first time on my bed. She bucked up in surprise. And then, to my surprise, she took to her knees, which granted me far easier access.

She wanted me to fuck her; I was in no doubt of that.

But it'd be better for us both if I just tasted her again first. I rolled over onto my back and slipped beneath her so as to lick those pretty folds of skin that sheltered her sensitive bud.

When I worked my way closer, I tasted her in my mouth and found her hard, blood-engorged clit. I licked around it and over it and around again, over and over. She rewarded me with her loud moans as she rubbed and thrust against my mouth.

Her movements became more frantic, and I sucked on her clit too. Her moans grew louder, urging me on. I knew she was about to come, and I wasn't about to stop.

My cock felt ready to burst. I was so turned on, and I didn't want this to end.

I pushed a finger inside her, just one. Moments later, her pussy quivered and clamped onto me. Her shouts became more shrill. Warm juice gushed from her, soaking my chin. And I thought there was a real danger I'd come too.

I held on to the base of my cock and just enjoyed it.

For a few seconds, she stayed perfectly still, and then she raised from my face by a few inches.

I escaped.

And she said, "Carl, please can you fuck me?" Thankfully I hadn't come.

I looked at my brothers and shrugged. Each of them grinned at me, and I realized I must have worn a stupid grin on my face too.

I shot over to my bedside drawer. Plenty of condoms in there.

Taking my eyes off the group on my bed was hard.

I hadn't known what my brothers were doing before, but now I saw their hands over her. I continued to watch.

She sat up a little, letting her legs support her weight, but she continued to crouch as she reached for each of their dicks and pulled them toward her. My brothers shuffled to where she wanted them.

The sight was mesmerizing. I had a perfect view of it all as she licked the crown of one and then the other.

I didn't think we'd need lube, she was so wet. But I didn't want to hurt her either, so after wrapping up, I added a blob of lube to my sheathed dick. I rubbed it around before kneeling behind her.

She hadn't changed position, so I guessed she wanted it like this.

Tentatively I worked a finger inside her and then two.

Her pussy was dripping with arousal, and her head continued to bob, swapping from one cock to another.

It was like watching porn — no.

Better.

It was like being in the hottest porn film I could imagine.

I eased my dick into her hot tight space and realized I wasn't made for porn because I doubted I could do this for long without shooting inside her.

She let go of my brothers' dicks as she needed her hands to support her weight. They could've held her if they'd have thought about it. Still, we could coordinate other positions in the future.

I was damned sure there would be plenty more times, and this wasn't a one-off. We were starting something that was going to get better and better.

Moving in and out with slow, gentle thrusts, I hoped I'd be able to hold off my climax until after I'd experienced the clamping of her orgasm around me, but I wasn't sure.

I wasn't sure of anything right then because I'd never experienced anything like it.

Not only had I never shared a woman with my brothers, we'd never even fucked in the same room, so this should've seemed pretty damned weird. But I was overwhelmed not just with lust, but with emotions I'd not experienced before.

I wasn't about to say it, but I felt overwhelmingly passionate about Sophie. I felt love for her. In love with her.

She was everything I wanted in a woman, in a girlfriend and lover.

The situation was incredibly erotic as two cocks found their ways to her mouth, and soon her pussy contracted in spasms on my dick. She came. I came. I withdrew.

I wondered if my brothers would take turns in my place, but Sophie asked them to come on her.

I sat back and watched.

She sucked both their dicks, holding one in each hand.

First, Ben put a hand out as a warning. "I'm going to come," he croaked, taking hold of his dick.

She aimed it at her breasts, the implication clear.

Adam followed his lead. Within seconds of each other, they coated her beautiful round tits with gooey white cum. It streaked over her, and in places, began to run down. They wiped their cocks through it, smearing it over her tits and her dark hard nipples.

I'd never been to a live sex show before. I was starting to think there were a lot of things I'd never done before.

I loved Sophie. I knew I did. And I loved watching her as the star of a private sex show with my brothers. It should've felt wrong. But it felt right.

They were all a mess, so I got up and got towels.

Sophie slept in my bed that night, but we didn't sleep for another hour or two.

First, we snoozed a little, then talked and finally played some more. Eventually, when it was almost morning, Adam and Ben slinked off to their rooms for a comfortable sleep. I briefly thought about how a bigger bed in my room might be required.

CHAPTER TWENTY
SOPHIE

When we finally made our second trip to Bunny's, the local diner, for breakfast, we were very much settled into our unusual relationship. It had been a few months, and our closest friends in college all knew about us.

I'd heard it said that people don't visit the things that are on their doorstep, usually referring to tourist attractions in their home cities. There was nothing closer to our home than Bunny's, but we more often frequented cafes further along the street. We usually ate at home because that worked well for us.

I was about to step into the diner for only the second time ever when I heard a female voice call out my name.

"Sophie!"

Carl tightened his arm protectively around my shoulder. We stopped, and Ben and Adam, who were walking behind, crashed into us. We laughed about that.

Most of the time, those boys were too close to me when we went out, so we often crashed into each other. I suspect it was deliberate half the time. I liked the way they were as drawn to me as I was to them.

I looked all around to see where the call had come from, and I spotted a woman waving at me from across the street.

We all stood and watched as she approached.

"Who is she?" I heard Ben whisper.

"No idea," Adam replied.

I couldn't instantly place the familiar face, but she recognized me and knew my name. We stood and waited while she approached. And as she got nearer, I remembered.

"Hi, Sophie."

"Hi, Elisha, this is Carl." We were still holding hands, so she probably guessed he was my boyfriend. Introductions would be awkward if explanations were required.

Ben and Adam were so close behind us; we hadn't stepped apart when we collided. I could feel hands on my back and at my waist, but Elisha wouldn't be able to see those. She could, of course, see that the guys all looked alike.

"This is Adam and Ben, hiding behind me."

I saw her looking at their faces, and I almost detected her brain whirring. It was obvious that they were triplets.

"And this is Elisha. I know her from college." I winked at her, hoping she wouldn't let on. I didn't want the guys to know that I'd considered moving out. We'd talk about it one day, but this wasn't the time or place.

"Sophie, it's you, isn't it?" She smiled a huge beaming smile, and I wondered what exactly she meant by stating the obvious. "I'd heard a girl is dating gorgeous triplets. The campus is buzzing with rumors. It is true, isn't it?"

Like all young people in love, we haven't exactly been overly discreet. The gorgeous triplets drew attention to themselves by merely being three handsome men who looked alike. Things that weren't exactly their fault.

Carl squeezed my hand.

I leaned my head on one side gave a wry smile. "It might be."

Her gaze swept over each of my guys.

"Don't worry, Sophie. You are the envy of every girl; let me tell you. And the rumors are true. They are gorgeous. It is true, isn't it?"

I nodded.

The guys were grinning and approving of the conversation. Their egos were already pretty big. To be honest, it had been a boost to my ego, knowing three gorgeous men wanted me and only me.

"Well, congratulations, Sophie. It looks like you did well. And I am dead jealous. Did I tell you my boyfriend is a twin?"

"You did, and that your brothers are twins."

"Really?" She looked puzzled. "That's right, I told you about my brothers, too. Actually, I'm meeting my brothers here."

"Would you like to join us?" asked Carl, which was typically sweet of him. "We can get a big table together."

"That'd be really nice, and another time I'd love to. It'd be fun. Today we need to sit alone for a family conference." She whipped out her phone and began tapping on the screen as she spoke. "In fact, Sophie, give me your number so we can fix something up for the future. We should arrange to get together."

I told her my number, and then my phone buzzed.

"I've sent you a message, so you have my number too. Now, let's go in and grab tables."

We moved toward the door, all of us allowing Elisha to go first when suddenly she stopped. "Are these guys also your stepbrothers?"

"Yes," we all said together.

Her eyebrows rose a little higher. "We really must talk soon. And you guys, be good to Sophie, or I'll send my brothers around to sort you out."

"She seemed to take that pretty well," Carl said after we'd ordered our food.

I agreed. "It's surprising, but most people do."

Adam raised his coffee. "Could be because we've only told other college kids. I'm not sure how older people would react."

"It doesn't matter what other people think, though."

It hadn't taken long for it to feel normal to us.

Our day-to-day lives didn't change as we continued to eat together and divide chores in just the same way as before.

I walked to college most often with Ben in the mornings, and between them, one of them would normally meet me to walk home in the evening. None of these things were different.

After we all had sex together and I truly lost my virginity, we talked a lot about the sort of relationship we wanted. It was difficult for me to comprehend and believe what they told me at first. We all agreed that we wanted a relationship that was exclusive between the four of us. I'd be their only lover, and they'd be mine.

"Do you hear how she says every girl envies me? They all think I'm getting a better deal out of this than you guys."

"Well, it's not true." Sitting next to me, Carl covered my hand with his.

"I can understand what they are thinking. I get three whole men, and you each only get a third of me."

"So you've got the worst deal. We all want your attention, so you have to work three times as hard to satisfy us, whereas we can be lazy." Ben chuckled.

I laughed too because, of course, it was nothing like that.

"Seriously, I get time to myself when I need it without having to feel guilty that I'm neglecting my girlfriend because I know there are two other guys taking care of you." Ben leaned in, so we all leaned closer toward him to hear. "And I don't believe I get less of you just because some nights you sleep with my other brothers."

"I like rotating between your three beds, so I never have to wash my sheets." I laughed and then added, "Or tidy my room." I had taken to spend each night with a different guy. Sex wasn't necessarily a part of that, but usually, it was.

Ben agreed, "Yeah, I looked in there. It's scary. There could be a family of homeless people making camp for all we know."

"And I don't think I only get a third of a woman," Carl whispered. "I can't believe how lucky I am that I get to make love to you on a one-to-one basis and enjoy all sorts of other sexy stuff that wouldn't be possible without more bodies in the room. As far as I'm concerned, this is the best relationship on earth."

"Yeah, too right." Adam was sitting opposite. Under the table, he wrapped his legs around mine. "When we do stuff that involves more than the two of us that's pretty mind-blowing too, I don't mind admitting."

The other guys nodded.

I bit my lip. What could I say? It was amazing for me.

"And I think there's a third thing that makes our relationship really work well for us brothers," Adam said. "You know I love you guys."

Ben gave Adam a shove. They were like eight-year-olds at times.

"Not in a weird way. We've always lived together and shared everything our whole lives. It would be strange for us to go our separate ways in our mid-twenties or thirties. I much prefer the thought of us living together with you. Not separately with three different women."

It wasn't the first time one of them had said something like that. It must've been a triplets thing, but it also said something about how they hoped this relationship would last into the future.

So did I.

"If we're going to continue, we'll have to tell our parents." I dreaded that. We'd gotten through Thanksgiving and Christmas, but I didn't think I could go through many more family gatherings faking and lying. "We should tell them soon."

Carl put his cutlery down on his plate and turned slightly toward me. "I know you're worried. I hope they'll be fine with it. We're not doing anything wrong. We're happy and in love and just a bit unconventional. It isn't a terrible thing."

We were sitting by the door, Carl and I with it in our line of sight, Adam and Ben had their backs to it.

We couldn't help but monitor everyone who came and went.

When the two guys came in, I noticed the police uniforms first. It seemed as if everyone went silent and looked in their direction, wondering whether they were there for business or pleasure. Had the owners called the police due to a crime taking place on the premises? Or were they coming in for breakfast like the rest of us?

Secondly, I noticed their faces, they were the spitting image of each other. They must have been brothers, and probably twins. They were looking around, and one of them soon focused on our table. Just as Adam and Ben looked around to see what we were looking at, Carl and one of the cops greeted each other.

"Hi, good to see you."

"Long time no see. Um," the policeman looked at all three of the triplets in a way that I now recognized was him working out who was who. This meant that he knew them well enough that he felt he could tell them apart, but didn't see them often enough for instant recall.

"Hey, Carl, Adam, Ben, we must meet up soon. We'll call you." They didn't stay long enough for proper introductions but departed, making their way toward the back of the cafe.

"How do you guys know them?"

"It's a long story, but not an interesting one."

I glanced around and watched where they went. "Elisha's brothers. They're cops."

CHAPTER TWENTY-ONE
ADAM

When we came out of Bunny's and made that short walk to our apartment, I had my arm around Sophie's shoulders. Briefly, we kissed on the lips. She may have been holding Ben's hand too as he stood on the other side of her.

Carl led the way. It might have been all of ten paces that we traveled before we stopped and waited for Carl to open the door.

We stopped and waited, and while she kissed Ben, I noticed our parents across the street with our younger sisters. They were all staring at us. We won't have to wonder when and how to tell them, I thought.

On impulse, I almost withdrew my hand quickly as if from a fire and stepped back.

I didn't.

I coughed.

Under my breath, muttered, "Don't look now because it's too late. Our parents are approaching."

I stood my ground because I was an adult, and I had made my choice about how I wanted to live and who I wanted to live with.

Carl turned around. "He's right."

Sophie wiggled from under my arm, and I believed she snatched back her hand from Ben. She suddenly looked pale and ill.

This may not have been the way our parents should have found out, but it was too late.

Younger sisters, being what they are, came right out with it as soon as they reached our side of the street.

"Have you got a boyfriend, Sophie?" asked Emma. Sophie's youngest sister stared at me as if she'd never seen me before.

"Are you dating all three because you can't tell them apart?" Megan asked, her gaze flitted between us.

Our sister, Diane, looked confused. "Okay, which of you guys is dating Sophie?" She sounded stern and put her hands on her hips as she spoke. It was comical for her age, but mostly for Sophie's sake, I didn't laugh.

Barbara's face looked like thunder.

Our father didn't look too happy either.

We lived in his apartment and had a few months left until we brothers completed our degrees. The gravity of the situation began to register with me. He wouldn't chuck us out or cut us off, I hoped. Could they split us up?

Carl stepped forward. "Let's talk up in the apartment, shall we, not on the street. And to what we owe the pleasure of this surprise visit?"

Silently, I thanked Carl for stepping in. He was the only one of us not caught with his hand in the proverbial cookie jar.

"We've come to pick up a new clarinet for Diane. Our journey took us through this neighborhood; we thought we'd just stop by."

TRIPLET TIME

"I did send you a text just a short while ago," Barbara said.

Sophie bit her lip. "I left my phone up in the apartment as we were just stepping down for some breakfast. I didn't think I'd need it."

I understood. I didn't have mine with me either because nothing else was as important to me as these three people. We'd all stopped bringing our phones to the dining table, and it was quite possible none of us had our phones when we stepped out together either.

The most important people in our lives were all together as a group. We had become a family and were making plans for our future together as one.

Ben and I had both secured positions for when we finish college in just a few months. Our jobs meant staying in the city. We envisioned continuing living in the apartment, assuming Dad didn't kick us out.

Carl hadn't found a job, yet he wasn't sure what he wanted to do.

While Sophie was still in the first year of her art degree, it seemed obvious to me that she and Carl could form an excellent business partnership related to the art world in the future.

Our father pulled out his wallet. "Girls, you go treat yourselves to whatever you want in there. And wait until we come back to fetch you." He handed Diane some notes. Enough for a week's worth of waffles, from what I could tell.

"You've got phones if you need us. Or we're in this building, top floor," Barbara said stiffly.

Carl unlocked the door, and we all followed in silence. We took the elevator in silence. We entered our apartment in silence. The longer it went on, the worse I felt about the way this was going to go.

In our apartment, Dad sat down at the dining table, and Barbara marched to the window.

This was good for us. My brothers and I positioned ourselves at various vantage points between them.

I'd learned something about the psychology of negotiation for my business degree, and it was something we'd discussed and played with at length as brothers. Already our opposition was divided, and nobody had said a word.

"What is going on?" Barbara demanded.

"We were just discussing how to tell you," Sophie replied. I didn't like leaving Sophie to face her mom like this but decided against intervening too soon.

"To tell us what exactly?"

Sophie looked over at me. Okay, it was time to step up after all. "We've been more than just roommates. We've been dating, and it's gotten serious," I replied.

"You and Sophie?" Barbara asked me directly.

For a moment, I wondered if we could pass it off as just one of us and Sophie. That might be easier for Barbara to accept. And here was when triplet telepathy would come in very handy. The damn thing didn't work for us.

I looked at Sophie. I knew that although she'd like to spare her mom from pain and anguish, lies made Sophie miserable.

"What we've got is unusual, but we all adore Sophie. We all love her."

I watched as Barbara drew in a sharp breath. Sophie sat down at the table with Dad. She looked shattered. I wanted to comfort her, but Carl moved first. He went and sat next to Sophie and placed his hand on hers.

"Sophie and I are dating, and I'm in love with her. She's dating Adam and Ben as well, and that's fine by all of us."

Ben moved to stand behind Sophie. "I'm in love with your daughter, Barbara. She's a special and unique girl, and I've never met anyone like her."

Understandably, Barbara was at a loss for words. I couldn't begin to imagine how she felt at that moment or what thoughts went through her mind.

I decided not to speak but give it time for the information to sink in.

"Sophie," our father's voice sounded calm and soothing. "What do you think about what my sons have said?"

She looked at him and replied, "It just happened, easily and suddenly. We got along so well living together that one thing led to another."

"They say they are in love with you. They haven't forced you into anything?"

Every one of us tensed. Anger rose inside me at the very suggestion. Could he imagine we were like that?

"No, absolutely not. I wanted them as much as they wanted me. It was mutual."

I turned to Barbara. "We promised to look after your daughter, and we have. Our living together arrangement works well, and we'd never let any harm come to her. Barbara, we three all sincerely love her. It might be difficult for you to understand, but we do."

She didn't even look at me. She did look at our dad. "What do you think of this?"

My heart sank. He'd just practically suggested something unthinkable and coercive was going on.

"Well, they've always been good boys. I had not one moment of doubt that Sophie would be safe when we moved her here."

Yes, Dad, exactly.

"And they are nice boys. They will make excellent husbands to future wives, so why shouldn't Sophie be one of those wives?"

"We don't want other wives. We aren't in an open relationship," said Carl. "We only want Sophie, no other women. We're faithful to her, and she is to us. We don't want to share her."

I knew what Carl meant, but it was a funny way of putting it.

A small smile came over my dad's face too. "Oh, I see. Just the four of you in a committed relationship?"

"Yes, sir."

"Polyandry, that's it. Is that what this is?"

We all nodded.

"I remembered the term for it. I knew a group of people once who had such a relationship. They may still be together, for all I know. If this is what you want, and it's working for you, then I have no problem with it."

I was both relieved and shocked. I looked at Barbara. She only looked shocked but not relieved.

"Barbara, Sophie was obviously going to date guys when she went to college. It seems to me she's picked three of the best guys the city has to offer and has decided to date them all at the same time. If they are all happy with that, then why should we have a problem?"

Barbara finally turned her attention to me. "How can you be happy sharing your girlfriend with other men?"

"I wouldn't be happy sharing a girlfriend with just any other men, and we've never done this before." Not that it was relevant or any of their business. "But the relationship I have with my brothers is special. We've got a tight bond. We'd trust each other with our lives. It's different."

Our dad stood up. "I think we should leave and talk about this between ourselves. I want to see you all happy, and if this makes you happy, then I'm good with that. We've got to collect the girls from the diner."

Barbara walked over to where Sophie sat. She leaned over and kissed Sophie on the forehead. "You'll always be my daughter, no matter what. I can't understand this at the moment. But I'll try."

CHAPTER TWENTY-TWO
SOPHIE

Cowardly I may be, but I was in no hurry to see our parents. I thought my boys, as I called them, felt the same.

When opportunities came around, we'd jumped at anything that ensured we had many reasons why we couldn't go home to visit them in Chester. There were always things to do to keep us in the city or reasons to go away any place but Chester. We booked a little trip away for Easter.

Mr. Cooper visited us from time to time. Ostensibly it was to deal with the apartment, which was why Mom didn't come with him. That excuse convinced no one. She had no reason not to spend a day out with him and see her daughter.

I didn't call Mom, and she didn't call me.

The boys spoke to their father regularly and networked with him over social media.

Mom and I made no effort to contact each other. Being an artist, I had acceptable methods of avoiding her. I made postcards out of my artworks and sent them to her on an almost weekly basis. We could both feel good about it. Me that

I'd made an effort. Her that she'd heard from me. And yet, we completely avoided direct communication.

When school finally broke up for the summer, and it was all over for my big boys, we set off on another trip.

We'd booked a private house for a beach vacation.

It was a long drive, but if we shared the driving and didn't stop for longer than it took to use the restroom, we thought we could get there within a long day.

We piled into Adam's car, and he drove the first shift. As I sat in the back with Carl and wasn't driving for many hours, I didn't pay too much attention to our route. After many miles, the view outside the window appeared all familiar.

We were exceptionally close to home. I knew for a fact that this involved a significant detour. Our hometown of Chester was not in the direct line of the coast.

"Who's idea was this?" I realized what they were planning, and I knew there was no point in getting upset about it. I could never stay cross with them for more than a few minutes. They always made me laugh or talk their way out of any trouble. They had a logical argument for everything, and it was impossible to win.

"Adam's driving, I'd say it's his fault," said Carl.

"I'm admitting nothing and denying everything," Adam called from the front.

Carl was sitting next to me; I aimed my comments at him. "You knew about it, didn't you? You're all in on it."

Carl breathed in deeply. Of the three of them, I knew he hated confrontation the most.

Ben turned around in his seat, "We're all agreed on this, so you're outnumbered, Sophie. You need to see your mom."

I sighed. "I'm not even going to argue with you because I know it's true. I just wish you would have warned me that this was the plan."

"It was for your own good. If we'd have warned you, you wouldn't have been excited about the vacation. You would have been worried about seeing your mom. As it is, we'll be there soon, so you don't have much time to think about it. We'll just get it over with quickly, and then we'll be on our way."

"How do you know she'll be there?" As I said it, I realized this plot was bigger than just the three of them. "Your dad is in on this too? Does Mom know we're coming?"

Carl shook his head. "No. Dad does, but not your mom."

"That's why I love you guys."

"Because we're so considerate, and we look after you in every aspect of your life?"

"Um, something like that."

When we pulled on to the driveway, I was surprised Mom came out to greet us. She pulled me into a big hug. "I've missed you," she whispered and more loudly added. "I've made some dinner, so I hope you kids are hungry. You always look like you need feeding."

Clearly, Mom was expecting us, but I didn't know when she'd learned we were coming.

"Where are the girls?" I asked after we'd settled in the kitchen with drinks and the delicious smell of home-cooked food teasing our senses. I wondered if they'd deliberately been sent somewhere to avoid us, so our freaky relationship couldn't corrupt their morals.

"They're at summer camp. They've been gone for a few days. I know they'll be sorry they've missed you, but they'd already left by the time I learned you were coming today. And it has been booked for ages."

Her lengthy excuse only made me more suspicious, not less. Nevertheless, Mom looked relaxed and genuinely happy to see us. There was no reason why she should be any different. We were the same people she knew last summer.

"Mom and Dad," Carl said, which was weird because she wasn't his mom. "We didn't just pop by to eat your food. There are a few things we wanted to tell you."

I looked at him and wondered what those things were.

"It's in no particular order of importance, so let's talk about me first." Carl chuckled. "I've decided to do a Masters in Art and Business studies." Judging by the looks on Adam and Ben's faces, this was news to them. "I've been offered a slot in the program, and I've decided to accept. I talked it through with Dad, so it's not news for everyone. I just wanted to tell you all."

I knew about the course and how much it interested him, but I didn't know he'd decided to go for it. I started clapping because, why not?

Adam and Ben both went over and gave him those brotherly handshakes that involve a lot of slaps on the arms and punches to the shoulders.

"So, it's my turn to make an announcement." Ben stood up and started to pace. "We've been dating Sophie for about ten months, and that's almost a year."

Their dad gasped. "It never is." I saw where they got their sense of humor.

"Strange but true," Ben retorted. "We wanted to do something special for our anniversary, and it would mean a lot to us if we could share it with you. If things were different, we'd ask Sophie to marry us, but that's not possible. Even so, this is a significant relationship for us all, and we want to share that with our family."

It was my turn to be amazed.

Ben didn't seem to notice exactly what he'd just said, but Carl and Adam both turned to look at me.

"What did you have planned, son?"

"We thought we'd have a party and invite everyone we know. Lots of people know us and think we're roommates, or aren't quite sure what's going on. So we thought a party to celebrate one year together as a group would be good."

"A group, rather than a couple. Is that what you call yourselves?"

"Um, we don't really call ourselves anything."

Ben looked at us for help, but he was right. We didn't have to give our relationship a name. It was what it was.

"Does that mean you've got an announcement too?" Mr. Cooper looked at Adam.

Ben sat down, and Adam stood up.

"Barbara, I think you have had doubts about our intentions toward your daughter. As we're brothers, very close brothers, we discuss stuff. And we've discussed Sophie a lot."

I wasn't sure what sort of discussions they might have had about me that were suitable to tell my mother.

He came over to me and took my hand. "Sophie, there isn't anywhere in the world where a woman can legally marry three men. We've looked into it because we're all agreed that if we could, that is what we'd like to do. We would ask you to marry us, and I hope you'd say yes."

I couldn't believe tears were welling up in my eyes at a hypothetical proposal of marriage. I felt foolish. I choked out the words, "I'd say yes."

The boys knew that just as I knew what they wanted.

We talked, and we lived together.

We knew what each other was thinking a good deal of the time.

"Dad, Barbara, we brothers wanted you to know how serious this relationship is to us. And Sophie," Adam turned back toward me. "We can't marry, but we can exchange rings and arrange our own ceremony to celebrate it. I speak for the three of us; we'd like to have four rings of significance made, one for each of us."

I nodded. I couldn't speak again.

Mom mopped a tear from the corner of her eye. "Rings are better than tattoos. I hear all you young people are getting each other's names tattooed these days."

Ben stood up; his face lit up with excitement, and his hands waved in the air. "Oh yes, tattoos. A list of our names. Why didn't we think of it?"

I knew he was teasing; we were not the type of family to go for matching tattoos, but he made us laugh.

Watch out for more of this group as they make an appearance in *Triplet Trouble, book 4 of the Triplets series*.

TRIPLET TATTOOS: #2 in Triplets series
TRIPLET TEASE #3 in Triplets series
TRIPLET TROUBLE #4 in Triplets series

Sign up to follow Stephanie on social media to get a notification when further books in the *Triplets* series are published.

Stephanie Brother is on Facebook and Instagram.

Printed in Great Britain
by Amazon